Gabby turned back temper with difficulty. 'I'm tired. I've had an incredibly long and trying forty-eight hours, and I'm wiped. Anyway, I thought you didn't want to entertain me.'

'I don't,' he said bluntly. 'It appears, however, that I don't have a choice.'

She tried again. 'Look, I don't like the idea of having to share your accommodation either, but we're just going to have to be civilised about it. I'm sure if we try hard we can manage to act like grown-ups,' she said sweetly, and, going into her room, she shut the door with a definite little click.

Dear Reader

'How about somewhere exotic?' my editor said. Exotic?
My brain isn't very good with exotic. The word always
makes me think of crowded beaches, millionaires and
weird-coloured drinks. 'How about an Indonesian
island?' I offered sneakily and promptly invented Pulau
Panjang. Well, it sounded exotic. It turned out to be far
from it, but it fitted with 'Changing Places', certainly
a change from England where we take modcons for
granted, and where culture means going to the opera, not
sitting three parts naked round an open fire smeared with
wood ash and eating fruit bats!

I grew up in Malaysia, and despite the mosquitoes, bats,
snakes and jellyfish it was a most glorious and enviable
childhood. I had absolute freedom because children are
sacred to the Malays, and I will never forget the kindness
of the people I met there, most particularly my nanny,
Rom, whom I ran ragged! She was wonderful. In fact,
just as soon as I can manage it, I'm going back with my
husband and children to see if I can find my island!

Caroline Anderson

CAPTIVE HEART

BY
CAROLINE ANDERSON

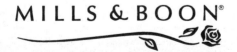

MILLS & BOON®

First published in Great Britain 1998
Harlequin Mills & Boon Limited,
Eton House, 18-24 Paradise Road, Richmond, Surrey TW9 1SR

© Caroline Anderson 1998

ISBN 0 263 81071 2

Set in Times Roman 10½ on 11½ pt.
03-9808-52007-D

Printed and bound in Norway
by AiT Trondheim AS, Trondheim

CHAPTER ONE

HE LOOKED like something out of an old B-movie.

Faded khaki shirt and shorts, feet propped up on the veranda, hat tipped over his face, chair tilted onto its back legs—and he was in the shade, which was another reason to dislike him on sight.

Gabby could feel the heat of the sun scorching down on her unprotected shoulders—the skin would probably be burned already. No doubt her nose was covered in a smattering of little freckles, with the rest of her programmed to follow in short order, but that was what you got for being a green-eyed redhead—sunburn and a lousy disposition!

She studied the man on the veranda again as she drew closer. As there was no one else around and no other dwellings in the vicinity, it must be him she was looking for, and he was every bit as clichéd close up as he'd been from a distance. She stifled a little laugh. She'd come all the way across the world and she'd stepped into the set of a Trevor Howard film, with the neighbourhood MO cast in the leading part!

He was quite well put together, however, despite the air of old-Colonial dissipation that hung over him. No doubt some Hollywood director would be thrilled to have him, she thought, examining him with clinical detachment. 'In fact, forget Trevor Howard,' she mumbled to herself, losing her clinical detachment, 'think Harrison Ford as Indiana Jones...'

His shirtsleeves were rolled up to expose deeply tanned and hair-strewn forearms, rippling with lean muscle, and long, rangy legs, strewn with more of the same gold-tinged wiry hair, stuck out of the bottoms of crumpled shorts. His feet were bare and bony, with strong high arches and little tufts of hair on the toes. They were at her eye level as she approached the steps to the veranda, and a little imp inside her wondered if they were ticklish.

She couldn't see his face because of the battered Panama hat tipped over his eyes, but his fingers were curled loosely around a long, tall glass of something that looked suspiciously like gin and tonic. The outside of the glass was beaded with tiny droplets of water, and in the unrelenting tropical heat it drew her eyes like a magnet. She swallowed drily and wondered if he'd mind if she pinched it.

Mind? Of course he wouldn't mind—he wouldn't know! He was fast asleep, a soft snore drifting out from under the hat at intervals—he looked so relaxed that Gabby had an insane urge to kick out the two legs of the chair on which he was balancing and knock him onto his indolent behind.

Only two things stopped her. One was her natural good manners. The other was the fact that he was a darned sight bigger than she was and would almost certainly get just a tad cross about it.

So she plopped down onto the edge of the wooden veranda, propped her back against the nearest post and cleared her throat.

Nothing. Not a flicker of reaction.

Damn. She was going to have to kick the legs—

'I'm asleep.'

She blinked at the deep growl that emerged from under the hat. She thought she saw the gleam of an eye, but she wasn't sure. He hadn't moved so much as a single well-honed muscle.

She swallowed. 'I know. I'm sorry. I hate to disturb you—'

'So why do it? I don't entertain bored tourists,' he drawled. 'It's not in my job description.'

'Well, excuse me,' she muttered under her breath. She stood up, banging the dust off her bottom and stomping down the steps, pausing on the rough track to turn and glare up at him. All she got for her pains was a view up the leg of his shorts which her grandmother wouldn't have approved of and which did nothing for her blood pressure.

'For the record,' she said tersely—petulantly? Probably. Oh, heck. She dragged her eyes away from his shorts. 'For the record,' she began again, 'I'm not a tourist, I'm Gabrielle Andrews—Jonathan's cousin. Penny sent me up here to tell you lunch will be ready—'

The chair legs crashed to the floor, making her jump, and he tipped back the hat with one finger and studied her out of startling blue eyes.

'In a minute,' she finished.

'Well, why didn't you say so?'

She scowled at him. 'I just did,' she said crossly.

His grin was lazy and did further damage to her blood pressure. So did his eyes, tracking equally lazily over her body and back to her face. That did it. She wondered if she looked as angry as she felt, standing there in the muddy road with her head tipped back at a crazy angle and her hair—the red hair that was a dead give-away for her temper—clinging to her forehead in sweaty tangles.

She brushed it impatiently back out of her eyes and glared at him. 'Well?'

'Well, what?'

'Are you coming?'

'To lunch?' He leant forward and propped his elbows on the railings, the cool, inviting glass dangling from those lean and very masculine fingers, and grinned that lazy grin again. 'Tell Penny I wouldn't miss it for the world. And by the way...'

'Yes?'

'You shouldn't stand about in that sun with your fair skin—you'll burn in seconds.'

Gabby had noticed. She stifled the little scream of frustration and smiled viciously at him. She thought she probably looked more closely related to a barracuda than to her mild-mannered cousin at the moment, but she was too hot and too cross to be nice—not to mention exhausted. 'Thank you. I had realised,' she retorted and, spinning on her heel, she walked back down the rough track to the bungalow where her cousin lived.

What a pain! Idle, indolent, laconic, self-serving pig! Doctor? 'Huh! Not in this lifetime,' Gabby muttered crossly.

Penny greeted her with a glass of something cold, tropical and absolutely delicious that improved her humour immediately. 'Mmm, yum,' she murmured, pressing it against her hot cheeks. She'd only been in the country since early that morning, and it would take her a while, she imagined, to get used to the heat. In the meantime, the icy glass felt wonderful—

'Did you find Jed all right?'

She stifled the urge to tell her cousin's wife what she thought of the cliché she'd found sprawled on the veranda. 'Yes—he said he'd come. I would have thought he'd be here now—he wasn't exactly busy.'

'I expect he'll be taking a *mandi*—a bath.'

Gabby blinked. 'In this heat? Surely he'd shower.'

Penny laughed. 'He hasn't got a shower—the bungalow's not that sophisticated, I'm afraid. He's using the *mandi* at the back of the bungalow—it's a bamboo enclosure with a big tank of water in it. You stand in it and bail water all over yourself out of the tank with a big scoop. Actually, it's wonderful.'

It sounded wonderful—more refreshing than the shower she'd taken just before she'd wandered up the road to call Jed for lunch, and which had already lost its impact in the tropical humidity.

Penny settled down beside her in the rattan lounger, took a long swallow of her drink and turned to face Gabby. 'So, how was the journey? You don't look too bad, considering how tired you must be. Are you sure you don't want to lie down?'

Gabby shook her head. 'I'm still too wound up. Perhaps later.' She thought of the flight from London to Kuala Lumpur, the two-hour stopover for fuelling, the short flight to Jakarta, and then stepping out onto the runway at the airport at two in the morning. It had been like walking into a sauna, and the five-hour wait with little Katie had been hot, smelly and at the wrong end of an exhausting journey.

They had had to transfer to the other airport for the local island service, and even in the middle of the night Jakarta had been seething. The airports had been crowded with travellers and they had spent the last couple of hours perched on their cases, dozing against each other.

That had been the easy bit. Their arrival shortly after dawn in the unbelievable crate in which they had made the last short leg of the journey had been nothing short of a miracle. Her heart had been in her mouth most of the way as she'd listened to the engine cough and splutter—

'So, how was the journey?' Penny asked again, breaking into her thoughts.

How was it? 'OK,' she replied, always the master of understatement. 'Although I would have had more faith in the last plane if I hadn't seen the pilot tinkering around under the engine cowling with a spanner just before we took off.'

Penny laughed. 'They're quite safe—well, mostly. Some of them are a bit rough, but it's not exactly a hot tourist route—well, not yet.'

Gabby looked around her. Below them, stretched out into the muddy estuary on stilts, was a bustling little wooden town, the shacks roofed with corrugated iron or palm leaves, the fishing boats tied up at the makeshift piers rocking gently in the swell.

A seedy hotel, a handful of shops, a bank and not much else comprised the westernised part of the town, legacy of the Dutch influence which had also been responsible for the few bungalows at the top of the hill, in one of which they were sitting. That was it, however. Behind them, just yards away, the jungle began and civilisation, such as it was, ended.

'Not exactly on the beaten track,' she agreed drily.

Penny laughed, and for a moment Gabby thought she sounded a little strained. 'Hence the resort. It's going to be very expensive and very exclusive, so we're told, and with minimal impact. That's why they want the hydro-electric power plant instead of generators—so they don't have the noise in the resort village.'

'Where will it be?'

Penny waved an arm at the little headland beyond the town. 'Over there, in the next bay. It's a fabulous spot, I can see the attraction for the tourists once it's done.'

'But not now,' Gabby said softly, instinctively reading Penny's unspoken words.

She shrugged. 'Perhaps not while it's quite so primitive. Jonathan loves it here, and the little ones are very happy. I just hope Katie settles down like the others have—I can't thank you enough for bringing her back to us.'

Gabby chuckled. 'She was no trouble at all—and, anyway, I got a free tropical holiday in the middle of winter out of it! What more could a girl want?'

'A swimming pool?'

'What, with a bar in the middle and some fancy waiter in a grass skirt, serving bizarre blue cocktails with parasols floating in them?' She shuddered theatrically, and Penny relaxed and smiled.

'Yes, they can be pretty tacky, some of those pools—and they aren't necessary really. The sea's wonderful if you don't mind the odd jellyfish. Still, sometimes I wonder if this doesn't go too far the other way. It will get busier, of course, once Jonathan's built the power station and we have real electricity—then the resort will get under way and prosperity will happen and, whatever they say, it'll get just like Bali in the end, which will be a shame in a way because it is beautiful like this, so unspoilt.'

'Will it be spoilt? I thought the developer wanted to keep it very low impact.'

She shrugged. 'He does. He's quite emphatic about that, but it might just open the floodgates for other firms to come in the slipstream, so to speak. He's supposed to have an arrangement with the government, but things change with time. Still, a little more civilisation wouldn't go amiss. It would be nice to be able to buy butter that wasn't rancid, for instance, but they haven't got a cold storage facility here yet, and they won't until they have a proper and reliable source of power.'

Gabby laughed. 'Something to look forward to.'

Penny shrugged. 'By the time they have I expect we will have moved on to another primitive site in Brazil or Africa.'

Was that a wistful longing Gabby could see in her eyes? 'Don't you ever wish Jonathan had a proper job—you know, nine to five, Monday to Friday, in Basingstoke or wherever?'

Penny smiled, and again for a second the strain showed. 'Of course, but he wouldn't be happy doing that so here we all are. If we didn't have Jed I'd probably refuse to live here, but having a doctor on the spot makes it much safer and there are wonderful hospitals in Jakarta and Singapore.'

Gabby thought of their 'doctor on the spot', and hoped no one was about to be ill. He looked much too laid-back to cope with anything faster than ingrowing toe-nails.

She remembered her last job, a three-month stint in A and E, and almost laughed aloud at the thought of Pulau Panjang's resident MO caught up the hurly-burly of real medicine. Still, what did she expect? No doctor worth his salt would give up a decent job to live out here quite literally at the edge of civilisation, if not somewhat beyond it—but, anyway, he was quite decorative in a rather rough-hewn sort of way so she could probably forgive him so long as she remained healthy!

The object of her musings ambled into view, dressed in equally faded but freshly pressed shorts and shirt, his dark blond hair still wet from his bath, and bounded up the veranda steps with a grin that, to Gabby's utter disgust, did stupid things to her insides.

He looked even more like Indiana Jones, and she regretted the weakness she had for the type. She thought of all the old-fashioned and appropriate words, like 'cad' and 'bounder' and 'rascal'—all oddly flattering. Damn.

He grinned at her, waggled his fingers and turned to their hostess.

'Hiya, Pen. How are you doing?' he said cheerfully

and, bending over, dropped a casual kiss on Penny's cheek.

She caught his hand and patted it. 'Hi, yourself. Can I get you a glass of juice?'

'I'll get it.' He wandered into the house and emerged a few moments later with a tall clinking glass and a jug. 'Top-up?' he asked the two women.

Gabby held her glass out and wondered if she hadn't judged him a little too harshly, but then he blew it all away by dropping into a chair, hooking his feet over the veranda and closing his eyes.

'Bliss,' he said with a muffled groan, and within seconds he was asleep. Gabby was astonished at the rudeness of the man. Didn't he have more respect for his hostess than to come for lunch and go to sleep?

'He's been up all night,' Penny said under her breath, as if reading Gabby's mind. 'Jon'll be here in a minute— I'll wake him up then.' She settled back in her chair, sipped her drink and levelled a searching look at Gabby. 'So, tell me about your job,' she demanded. 'Got anything lined up yet?'

Gabby shrugged. 'Not yet. I don't want to go back to London, and there's nothing in my line anywhere else at the moment.'

Well, there was, but she would have had to cancel her holiday to attend the interview and wouldn't have been able to escort little Katie home. After the bout of appendicitis which had struck Katie while they had been on leave Gabby's temporary lack of employment had seemed like a godsend. It had meant that Katie hadn't had to travel alone once she was fit—for which service, Gabby reminded herself, she had been well paid despite all her protests that it wasn't necessary.

And there was no way she would have passed up the opportunity to see this wonderful tropical island, a tiny jewel in the Indonesian archipelago. Called Pulau Panjang, or Long Island, in Bahasa, the universal language of Indonesia, it was easy to see why from a map—and indeed from the air. Several times longer than it was wide, her first view had been of a huge, vivid green crescent in the turquoise sea.

As the ancient little plane had circled overhead she had had the most spectacular view of the thick unbroken green of the jungle with its winding rivers, slicing through the hillside on their way down the mountain, the deserted sandy coves and the isolated little settlements scattered here and there.

It was like something out of *Robinson Crusoe*, she'd thought, only bigger, and then at one end, clustered round an estuary, she'd spotted a larger settlement with an airstrip no bigger than a pencil line.

Around the town there was a terraced area of *padi* fields where she was told the locals grew rice and soya beans in rotation, but apart from that there was little sign of cultivation on the island. Because of the shape it was also known as Pulau Pisang, or Banana Island. Apparently, so Penny told her, Indonesian places often had more than one name, which just added to the delightful confusion.

The airstrip lay to the south of the town, on a spit of land sticking out into the sea, and although it was a little bigger than it had appeared from the air it was still barely adequate. What would happen if the plane failed to stop didn't bear thinking about, but it was hardly a jet. The little twin-engined monstrosity would probably just bellyflop into the sea and be towed back to land by a group of cheerful Indonesian children, yelling, 'Hello, Mister!'

It was the sum total of their English, apart from 'Give me money, give me sweets', which was the tail end of the refrain she had heard ever since her arrival in Jakarta that morning. Katie had been wide-eyed. For Gabby, it summed up the influence of the west on the innocent children of the east, and she felt faintly ashamed.

This island, though, had been unlike that, the children simply friendly and curious and the adults likewise. They had been courteous, voluble and charming—which was more than could be said for the company doctor.

A soft snore rippled the air, and she glowered at him and willed him to wake up and not just lie there.

She got her way. As she watched, his fingers relaxed their grip on the almost full glass of juice and ice and it tipped up on his chest. He gave a startled yelp and sat up, blinking and swatting at his shirt, but the damage was done.

That'll teach you, Gabby thought, stifling a laugh, but she was the one who suffered in the end because he stripped off his shirt, mopped the hair-tangled expanse of his deep, muscular chest with the soggy bundle and dropped back into the chair with a sigh.

'I suppose you want another one,' Penny said with a grin.

He flashed her a smile full of wry self-disgust, and to her horror Gabby found herself warming towards the rogue.

'Shirt or drink?' he asked ruefully. 'It was my last clean shirt. Last night was a bit heavy on them.'

Penny stood up. 'I'll get you one of Jon's. Can't have you frightening the natives—or Gabby. Help yourself to the drink.'

She left them, and Gabby felt his eyes graze her skin, sending a shiver over it. 'I don't think I frighten you, do I, Gabrielle?' he murmured, his voice a little husky. 'Rather the opposite, I feel.'

She blushed and glared at him, and he chuckled, a

deep, warm sound that was nearly as attractive as the expanse of bronzed skin that filled Gabby's line of sight. She shifted slightly and turned her eyes to the little town below them, the houses clustered along the curve of the bay and stretching up towards the brilliant green of the terraced *padi* fields.

She hoped he would leave her in peace, but no chance. That deep, slightly husky voice teased at her senses again like a caress. 'Pretty, isn't it? Especially if you don't have to live here.'

She turned back to him and tried to avoid ogling his body. 'Don't you like it?'

He shrugged. 'It's where the work is. You do what you have to do.'

Like sleep on verandas. Gabby was less than sympathetic, and it probably showed, but she really didn't care. As far as she was concerned, what he seemed to be doing couldn't possibly be construed as work. She thought of the sick people of the world, and of him passing the prime of his life with his feet on the railing of some tropical veranda, and despaired of the waste of talent.

If he was, indeed, talented. Perhaps he'd been struck off?

'How long are you here for?' he asked after a pregnant pause that she refused to fill.

'Three weeks—and, don't worry, I won't expect you to entertain me.'

He said something under his breath—not an apology, she was sure. She turned and met his eyes, her own glittering with challenge, and that sapphire gaze locked with hers. The same sparkling blue as the tropical sea beneath them, they issued their own challenge.

'That's just as well,' he said mildly. 'I'm much too busy to play nursemaid to a tourist—even if she is related to the boss.'

'Busy?' Gabby couldn't keep the scepticism out of her voice, but he either chose to ignore it or it went over his head, which she doubted. Most likely he had a skin like a rhinoceros.

Penny re-emerged, clean shirt in hand, sparing them the necessity of any further conversation. He stood up and pulled it on, and Gabby noticed with interest that it was a little on the tight side, compared to his other one. Not surprising, really. He was somewhat larger than her cousin, better muscled—heavens, she must stop looking at his body!

She was just wondering how she was going to get through lunch, without disgracing herself by being rude or ogling him, when a Jeep appeared on the horizon, horn blaring, bearing down on them in a hurry.

With a muffled exclamation Jed was on his feet and running over the lawn to meet the Jeep before it came to a halt. Penny and Gabby followed a little more slowly, and arrived at the Jeep to see Jonathan in earnest conversation with Jed.

'Just serviced two days ago,' Jonathan was saying worriedly. 'I can't understand it.'

'Where are the men?'

'Up at the compound. I didn't think it was safe to move them without you. Derek's giving them first aid.'

'Right. I'll get some gear. What injuries are we talking about?'

He was getting into the Jeep, and Gabby put a hand on Jonathan's arm. 'Can I help?' she asked.

'I hardly think this is going to be a spectator sport,' Jed growled, but Jonathan ignored him.

'Thanks. Get a hat and put on something with sleeves—we'll pick you up shortly. Oh, and wear sensible shoes.'

She ran back to the bungalow with Penny, opened her

case and pulled out thin cotton trousers, a long-sleeved cotton shirt and trainers. She was back in the road in seconds, Penny following her to plonk a hat on her head, and as the Jeep came careering past she jumped in before the vehicle had even come to rest.

'Pity about lunch,' Jed said. 'You should have stayed and kept Penny company.'

Jonathan, she noticed, was missing. Ignoring Jed's barbed remark, she asked where her cousin had gone.

'Phoning for an air ambulance to take the men out—sounds like it might be necessary. God knows why you wanted to come—I expect it'll be somewhat gory. Just keep out of the way and don't faint on me, all right? I don't need any more casualties and if you're anything like your cousin you'll go green at the first drop of blood.'

'I think I can cope,' she told him drily. 'After three months in A and E as staff nurse, I'm sure one more accident won't turn my stomach.'

His head snapped round and he stared at her in amazement. 'You're a nurse? God, woman, why didn't you say so?'

'You didn't ask—and don't call me "woman".'

A brow climbed into his hairline, and those full, firm, well-shaped lips quirked at the corners. 'Yessir,' he said with a grin. 'Right, hang on tight, it gets a bit rough here.'

For the next twenty minutes she was heartily relieved that she didn't have a roof over her head because she would have smacked into it countless times. She was also glad that she hadn't had her lunch. 'A bit rough' turned out to be the understatement of the century.

'The road's the next thing on the list, once we've established where the plant's going to be,' he yelled over the scrabbling of the tyres and the grinding roar of the engine. 'Obviously we can't do anything in the way of construction with the road like this, but until the feasibility study's been completed there's no point.'

Gabby just hung on and wondered if anyone had done a feasibility study about staying in bouncing Jeeps at fifty miles an hour on jungle tracks.

And it really was jungle, she realised when the mud forced Jed to slow down enough for her to focus on her surroundings. All around them the trees soared skywards to the canopy, their trunks straight and tall and leafless, and at the edges of the road the undergrowth was rioting in the light and air let in by the narrow channel the road had cut through the canopy.

She didn't recognise a single plant—not that she was much of a botanist but, even so, she was surprised that things were so strange and different.

'What's happened to the men?' she asked belatedly.

'Nobody's quite sure. They were driving back from town this morning and crashed.'

She wasn't surprised. It didn't take a genius to work out that the road was dangerous. They passed the tangled remains of a Jeep in the undergrowth on a bend, and then suddenly she could see light and they were in a clearing. Wooden prefabricated huts clustered round a central square, and Jed slid to a halt outside a hut labelled somewhat grandly INFIRMARY just as the rapidly blackening sky opened.

Gabby gave a little shriek as the first fat, heavy drops hit her, and then Jed was jumping out of the Jeep and telling her to hurry. 'Bring the rest, could you?' he yelled, and then, grabbing bags and boxes of equipment, he ran up the steps and inside, leaving Gabby to follow. She straightened her hat, scooped up the last remaining supplies and went after him at a run.

It was like an oven inside, and the sound of rain on

the tin roof was deafening. She looked out of the window and saw it fall in a solid sheet, flattening the exposed plants at the edge of the clearing and turning the area to a sea of mud in seconds. She felt sweat break out on her skin and run in rivers down her spine, and she longed for a cool shower or the *mandi* Penny had spoken about. No time for that, though, there was work to be done.

The hut was dimly lit, with four beds arranged around the single room. Men lay on three of them with others clustered around, trying to help. Two seemed reasonably comfortable, if a little bloody. The third, the one Jed had gone straight to, looked awful. A young Indonesian, he was pale and sweating, his lips were blue, his eyes were rolling and he was obviously very seriously injured.

'Thank God you're here,' an Englishman yelled over the noise of the rain. Derek presumably, Gabby thought. About thirty years old, lean and bespectacled, he was covered in blood and dirt, and he looked harrassed and weary. 'Right out of my league,' he continued. 'I'll go and tell Ismail to bring boiled water. Anything else you need?'

Jed shook his head and bent over the man, examining him quickly. 'Chest,' he said economically, and proceeded to sound it, his face impassive. 'Tension pneumothorax—we'll have to put a drain in before we can move him. I've got some stuff in there somewhere that we can use.'

'I'll set up—you check the other two,' Gabby said quickly. 'Is there somewhere I can wash?'

He rattled off instructions in Bahasa, and one of the men left the room and reappeared moments later with a bowl, fresh water and a towel that looked reasonably clean. She used one end and left the other for Jed, and went back to prepare their patient.

She knew where he would want to enter the chest wall, and she swabbed and wiped it, washed it with io-dine solution and left it to dry while she fished around in the bag he'd shown her. All she could find of any use was a urinary catheter, some tape, a couple of pairs of rubber gloves, a scalpel, a pair of scissors and some local anaesthetic and suturing equipment.

She drew up the lignocaine into one of the syringes, recapped the needle and turned to him. 'Ready when you are.'

He nodded, came over and checked the things she'd set out on a sterile paper towel and then injected the local into the area around the fourth rib space, before washing his hands. Gloved up, he swabbed the area again, sliced neatly with the scalpel and then inserted the point of the scissors, twisted and opened.

There was a hissing sigh of air out of the chest cavity, and behind them a dull thunk over the noise of the rain. 'Hello, one of the boys has bitten the dust,' Jed said softly. 'Can we find a bottle of water to put the end of the catheter in? Boiled water, tell them.'

'I can't,' she reminded him, handing over the catheter. 'I don't speak a word of Indonesian.'

There followed another stream of instructions, thrown over his shoulder as he deftly pushed the catheter in, taped it to the chest wall and stood up. 'Right, let's get this air out.' He pushed gently on the chest, listening to the sighing exhalation of air from the tube, and as he released the pressure he folded the end of the tube over to prevent air re-entering the chest cavity.

Immediately their patient started to look better. His colour improved, and he groaned and his eyes fluttered open. '*Obat*,' he whispered.

'What's that?'

'Medicine—he wants some painkiller, I expect.' She

drew up a shot of pethidine while he spoke quietly to the man in his own language, running his hands lightly over the bruised and battered limbs and gently palpating the abdomen.

'Seems to be fairly all right, apart from the chest and a broken arm. I'll just check the others again—give him the pethidine and watch him, would you?'

He turned to the man who'd fainted on the floor behind them and was now coming round, leaving her to her own devices. Gabby found herself lost without a language in which to communicate so she spoke in English, murmuring gentle reassurance. It seemed to work. The man relaxed his death grip on her hand, but when she soothed his head and touched his forehead his eyes widened.

'Careful—the head is sacred. You never touch it unless you've asked permission, and never with your left hand—it's an insult. Never take or give anything with your left hand, either. Always use the right.'

Jed's quiet advice made her aware of how little she knew. How could she really be of help amongst these people about whom she knew nothing? She could offend so easily without any idea of what she had said or done. Perhaps she should just go outside, sit down and wait for him before she did something truly awful—

He was beside her again. 'Don't get bent out of shape—it doesn't matter. I'll explain.' He broke into the native tongue again, and the man relaxed and almost smiled.

A few moments later Jed beckoned to her and they went out onto the veranda. The rain had stopped, and the air was cooler and fresher. It felt wonderful. She turned to Jed. 'Sorry about that—I didn't realise about the head. What did you say to him?'

His grin was wicked and did silly things to her insides. 'I told him you were a healer. Healers can do anything.'

She gave a hollow laugh. 'I wish. It would come in awfully handy sometimes.'

'Tell me about it,' he muttered. 'Right, we need to get these limbs splinted up for the journey down to the airstrip. Both these others have got fractures—one arm, one leg.'

They worked side by side without comment, strapping limbs to makeshift splints made of bits of wood wrapped in clean towels. They padded them and supported them as well as they could, but even so Gabby knew it was going to hurt, bouncing down that hillside to the town.

They laid two of them in the back of the Jeep, but the third, the man who had the chest drain, Jed propped up on the front seat between them so Gabby could keep an eye on him and the bottle of water as they travelled slowly and carefully down the hill.

It took nearly an hour, almost three times as long as it had taken to drive up, and when they arrived they could see the little plane just taxiing to the end of the runway. Jed drove along the edge of the strip to the plane, and then they loaded their patients, handed them over to the medical crew and sent them off to Jakarta for treatment.

As they watched the little plane climb into the sky and bank away towards Jakarta, Jed turned to her. 'Thank you for your help—it was invaluable,' he said quietly. 'Most things I can manage on my own, but there are times like this when a skilled assistant makes all the difference.'

She felt heat brush her already warm skin, and looked away, confused by the sudden rush of pleasure his words had given her. 'It was nothing—I only did what I'm trained to do,' she replied diffidently.

'Nevertheless, you did it well. Thanks.'

A silly grin crept onto her lips and she turned away, walking back to the Jeep so that he wouldn't see her response. Why would those few words of praise mean so much?

Because he was competent and skilled himself, of course. She'd seen that in the quick, precise movements of his hands, the assessing eyes, the searching fingers—he was a natural physician, and his praise did matter.

She grinned again, and swung up into the Jeep. 'Get a move on, I'm hungry,' she told him as he ambled up.

'Typical woman—always complaining.'

'Typical man—always providing something to complain about,' she returned.

It was almost four o'clock when they got back to Jonathan's and Penny's house, and as Gabby went to have a shower and change into clean clothes she heard Jonathan and Jed in conversation.

They were talking in low tones about the accident, too quietly for her to grasp more than the general drift, but one word jumped out of the urgent exchange.

Sabotage...

CHAPTER TWO

LUNCH turned into an early supper.

They sat on the veranda and ate their delayed meal of cold chicken in spicy sauce, rice and avocado salad and wonderfully exotic fruit. It was delicious, but Gabby couldn't concentrate on it. She was too tired to enjoy the food, and all she could think about was the three injured men who had been airlifted to hospital, and the possibility that their injuries had been caused deliberately.

It was the sole topic of conversation, in any case.

'It seems that the brakes failed,' Jonathan told them. 'The driver told Derek that they were working one minute, and the next there was nothing there at all. He was completely helpless. You know that stretch of road—all hills and bends. It's lethal enough with brakes. Without them it's suicide.'

Jed frowned. 'Has anybody checked out the vehicle?'

Jonathan shook his head. 'No, not yet. Derek's going to do it now.'

'But surely it could just have been a simple failure. Why would anybody want to tamper with the brakes?' Gabby asked, puzzled.

'To frighten us off?' Jonathan suggested.

'But why?'

'That's what we don't know,' he replied. 'It's the third or fourth incident in the past couple of weeks. The first was nothing much—a generator was smashed. It was irritating vandalism, we thought. Perhaps some of the boys from the town out looking for mischief. Then the cookhouse was burned down. It could have been an accident—a spark lodged in the roof or something. Then one of the Indonesian engineers left suddenly without explanation. We still don't know why, but he seemed very frightened and it spooked the others.'

'And now this,' Gabby said thoughtfully.

'And Mohamed last night.'

They looked at Jed. 'Mo?' Jonathan said. 'I thought he slipped and fell?'

'But why? He won't talk about it. By the time he went out on the plane this morning he was still refusing to discuss it, and he seemed scared. I think he either saw or heard something, or someone pushed him. Whatever, I don't think he just fell down that cliff.'

Penny licked her lips nervously. 'But why? Why are they being targeted? Do they want us to use workmen and engineers from the island?'

'Or do they just want us to go away?' Jed said quietly.

'But why?' Penny asked again. 'What are we doing that's upsetting them?'

Jonathan shoved his hands through his hair and sighed. 'Lord knows, darling; but I don't think you need to worry. It seems to be restricted to the Indonesians at the moment—I think it must be some local thing. There's a lot of rivalry between the different areas, but I'm sure we're all quite safe.'

Gabby shot Jed a look and saw him shake his head slightly, as if in mute disagreement. Did he think they were in danger?

She didn't have a chance to find out because at that moment the children finished their nap and came and joined them, and the topic was dropped instantly. Later, though, a messenger came from the compound and Jonathan excused himself and left, his face troubled.

Jed went too, and Gabby, exhausted from her trip,

suddenly ran out of steam. 'Penny, I need to go to bed,' she told her hostess.

'Oh, heavens, how dreadful of me, you must be exhausted!' Penny exclaimed. 'Oh, Gabby, I'm so sorry. I'll take you up there now.'

'Up?' she asked, puzzled. There was no 'up' in the bungalow.

'To the guest house. I'm afraid you'll have to share it with Jed,' she said apologetically, 'but it's got two quite separate bedrooms and a large living area and veranda in between. I don't think you'll be too much on top of each other. It's just that both our bedrooms in this house are already overstretched, but it's a very nice bungalow—I'm sure you'll be quite comfortable.'

Share. With Jed.

Great.

She dredged up a smile, heaved her case off the veranda steps, swung her flight bag over her shoulder and followed Penny up the uneven road to the bungalow where she had found Jed that morning.

'Rom has made your bed up ready—if you want anything just ring and one of the servants will come and see to you. We all eat at our house—it's got the only decent kitchen. Make sure you put plenty of insect repellent on—and have you started a course of anti-malarials?'

Gabby nodded. 'Of course. So's Katie.'

'Oh, yes. Right. Well, here you are...'

She threw open the door of a plain but spotlessly clean room. The windows were open but had mesh screens over them, as did all the doors and windows, and there was a fan on the ceiling that creaked slowly into life when Penny pushed a switch.

The bed was made up with crisp white sheets, and dangling over it was a thick, net rope suspended from the ceiling.

'That's a mosquito net—you spread it out and tuck it into the edge of the mattress when you go to bed. It cuts the air circulation down a bit, but it's better than being eaten alive and, although the screens help, the odd bug gets in through the doors. When the power station's built we'll get air conditioning, of course, but the generator can't manage it.'

Gabby didn't care about air conditioning. She just wanted to get her head down and get some sleep. First, though, she was going to explore the *mandi*.

She opened her case, found a cool cotton nightshirt and some fresh underwear, grabbed the thick white towel off the end of the bed and padded out to look for the bathroom.

There was a loo and basin off a corridor at the back of the bungalow, but the *mandi* was located, as Penny had said, outside the back door. There was a wooden walkway and a bamboo structure like a little shed, and she opened the door and peered in.

A cold stone floor and a big tank of deliciously cool water convinced her she wanted to try it. She shed her clothes and looked about for somewhere to put them, but there didn't seem to be anywhere. 'Oh, well,' she shrugged, put them on the floor in the corner, piled the fresh ones on top and tipped a scoop of water over her head.

A little shriek escaped before she could control it, but she was expecting the next scoopful. It was cold against her hot skin, but wonderfully refreshing. There was a bar of soap that smelt like Jed, and she rubbed it over her body and wondered if he'd done the same.

What a curiously intoxicating thought, she thought, humming cheerfully. Strangely intimate.

She rinsed, grabbed the towel from over the door and

rubbed her hair, threw it back out of her eyes and then looked at her clothes.

Soaked. Not just damp, but sodden. She must have been flinging the water around with even more abandon than she'd realised!

Oh, well, there was no one about. She wound the towel around her body and tucked it in over her breasts like a sarong, scooped up her soggy clothes and went back inside.

It was getting dark rapidly now at the end of the day. The light was fading fast, night literally falling, plummeting her into a velvet blackness.

She paused for a moment, listening to the sounds of the night from the jungle behind her, and a shiver went down her spine.

Primeval forest, full of strange plants and even stranger creatures. She felt as if someone was watching her, and a shiver ran through her again. Clutching the towel tighter round her, she hurried inside.

The bungalow was gloomy without lights, the rooms almost completely dark now, so the sudden movement of a white-clad figure startled her. With a little scream she stepped back, thumped her heel against a low table and sat down on it with a bump.

'Feeling a little jumpy?' Jed said mildly.

She swore somewhat colourfully under her breath, and rubbed her heel. 'Where did you come from?' she snapped. 'I didn't hear you drive up.'

She could hear the laughter in his voice, though. 'I'm not surprised, with all the splashing and singing,' he teased. 'I gather you enjoyed it.'

She hoped it really was dark and that it wasn't just her eyes because she could feel the heat scorching her cheeks. Had she really been singing? Oh, Lord.

'It was wonderful, but my clothes got wet.'

'You're supposed to take them off—'

'On the floor,' she said drily.

'Before you go in.'

'Oh.' She had a sudden vision of Jed going to the *mandi* stark naked, and the colour in her cheeks grew yet brighter—just as he flicked the lights on.

'You've caught the sun,' he said softly, bending to brush her burning skin with his knuckles. The light touch against her cheeks sent a tiny shock wave through her, and she stood up, dodging past him, and went to her room.

'I'm going to bed,' she told him. 'I'll see you in the morning.'

'Running away?' he asked with gentle mockery.

She turned back to him, hanging onto her temper with difficulty. 'I'm tired. I've had an incredibly long and trying forty-eight hours, and I'm wiped. Anyway, I thought you didn't want to entertain me.'

'I don't,' he said bluntly. 'It appears, however, that I don't have a choice.' His face was stony and he was clearly unimpressed, but there was nothing she could do about it.

She tried again. 'Look, I don't like the idea of having to share your accommodation either, but we're just going to have to be civilised about it. I'm sure if we try hard we can manage to act like grown-ups,' she said sweetly, and, going into her room, she shut the door with a definite little click, looked for a bolt and was disappointed.

Well, she'd just have to rely on his good manners— if he had any. So far she hadn't seen much evidence of them, but she'd give him the benefit of the doubt for now. She was too tired to do anything else.

She dragged a comb through her hair, spread a dry towel over her pillow and lay down on the bed, arranging the mosquito net over herself as Penny had said.

It was the last conscious thing she did for eleven hours.

'Tea, mem.'

Gabby's eyes struggled open and she sat up, fighting the layers of mosquito net that were tangled round her.

'Come in,' she called, and the door swung open to admit a young Indonesian girl with a smiling face and a very welcome pot of tea on a tray.

'Where's Jed?' she asked, wondering if it was safe to use the *mandi*.

'*Jalan-jalan*,' the girl replied, and then with a little bob and a smile she was gone, leaving Gabby with her tea.

She wondered where Jalan Jalan was. The compound? The town? She looked at her watch, and discovered it was six o'clock. Plenty early enough not to worry, she thought, and sipped her tea with gratitude. It was flavoured with the powdered milk she was beginning to get used to, and which she dimly remembered from a short spell in Sarawak in her early childhood.

She looked out of the window and saw that it was light again. Wonderful. She felt better—positively energetic. She disentangled herself from the mosquito net, stripped and wrapped herself in a towel and went out to the *mandi* for another delicious slosh around.

This time she managed to get back to her room without being caught, and she dressed quickly and went down the road to Penny's and Jonathan's bungalow. There the same girl who had brought her tea informed her that *Tuan* had gone out and *Mem* and the children were still in bed.

'*Doktor* come back,' she was told and, looking over her shoulder, she saw Jed strolling up the road from the town, a string bag dangling from his fingers.

'Morning,' he called, and she went down off the veranda towards him.

'Morning. I gather you've been to Jalan Jalan—is that the town?'

He laughed, showing even white teeth that gleamed against his tan. '*Jalan-jalan* means to go for a walk but, you're right, I have been to town. I wandered down to the market in Telok Panjang for some fruit. Join me for breakfast?'

Join Jed? She was astonished at the invitation after last night's cool rebuttal, but she was starving and it sounded wonderful. 'Sure you've got enough?'

He grinned, showing those teeth again. 'If I ate all this lot I'd be really ill,' he said with a chuckle.

Gabby fell into step beside him, thinking that if she wasn't so busy being critical of him professionally she could probably enjoy the man's company—and why was she thinking that? He'd already made it clear how unwelcome her presence was, from the comment about entertaining tourists through to his lack of enthusiasm the night before over having her as a house guest.

She was probably the last person he'd seek out as a companion—and, anyway, she wouldn't want him to because she couldn't separate Jed the doctor from Jed the Hollywood cliché. She'd seen him at work the day before, after all, and knew he was capable of working efficiently and well—so why wasn't he?

Unless, of course, they were going to continue to have accidents like that one, in which case his expertise would be well and truly put to the test.

'Did you find out what happened about the brakes?' she asked as they climbed the veranda steps.

His face clouded. 'No. The Jeep was burned out.'

She frowned. 'No, it wasn't. We saw it.'

'They must have done it after we came down again

with the casualties. When Derek went to look at it, it was a heap of smouldering ash. They were lucky there wasn't a forest fire, but I suppose the rain would have made it safer by damping everything down.'

'Damping?' She laughed, thinking of the slashing torrents of water that had fallen. 'Does it always rain like that?' she asked, amazed yet again that the sky could hold such vast quantities of water.

Jed grinned. 'Every afternoon. That's the beauty of it—you can get about in the sun in the morning, even in the monsoon season. It just makes the mud a bit deeper and the roads even worse.'

That was hard to imagine. The thought of the track up to the compound getting any worse was mind-boggling. She just hoped she wouldn't have to travel it again if it did.

She followed him into the kitchen area at the back, and he washed the fruit, piled it into a bowl, picked up two plates and some knives and spoons and headed back to the veranda, leaving her to bring from the fridge the glasses of juice he had poured.

They settled themselves down on the veranda out of the direct heat of the sun, already scorching at only eight in the morning. The fruit looked wonderful, and Gabby realised she was ravenous. She had hardly eaten anything the day before, and it seemed for ever since she'd had a decent meal.

'What's this?' she asked, picking up a fuzzy little pinkish red fruit.

'Rambutan—it means hairy. Just peel it and eat it, but be careful. There's a stone inside.'

She pulled off the skin, bit into the translucent white flesh and sighed with delight. 'Oh, wow.'

He chuckled. 'Lovely, aren't they? I managed to get a couple of mangosteens, too,' he said, proffering a dark purple ball the size of a small orange. 'It's a bit early in the season for them, but one of the traders owed me a favour. Crush it in your hands to split the skin, then it's easy to peel.'

Gabby found herself wondering what sort of favour he'd been owed as she peeled one of the precious mangosteens, then promptly forgot to worry about it as she tried the fruit. Segmented like an orange and with firm white flesh like the rambutan, it, too, tasted wonderful. Silently thanking Jed's favour-owing friend at the market, she moved on to sample a wedge of mango, a slice of papaya and a pomelo, before admitting defeat.

'I'll be ill if I have too much before I'm used to it,' she said and, sipping her drink, she lay back in the chair and opened her mouth to quiz him about local customs.

She didn't get a chance, though, because he smacked down his glass and stood up with lazy grace.

'Right, I must get on. See you later—and don't forget to cover up if you go out, remember to take your anti-malarials and drown yourself in insect repellent—and don't go near the jungle. There are snakes.'

'Yes, Mum,' she replied, trying not to look at those well-made legs only inches away from her face.

'Just doing my job as camp MO,' he said mildly, then left her to it, bounding down the veranda steps and heading off towards a battered old Jeep. It started with a cough and a rattle, and set off up the road with a little spurt of dust. The clutch was obviously less than subtle—or else it was Jed's driving.

She leant back, closed her eyes and dozed for a while, then Penny came and found her. 'Hi. How are you feeling?'

'Tired—it hit me last night and my system's all confused. All I want to do is sleep!'

'So sleep. We aren't doing anything today—Jon wants

to sort out this business of the crash yesterday, put out a few feelers. I'm sorry you had to go and work when you're supposed to be on holiday. It was very kind of you.'

She dismissed the remark with a wave. 'It was nothing. I couldn't sit here and twiddle my thumbs and let people bleed to death, could I?'

Penny laughed. 'No, I suppose not. Why don't you come down and spend the day with me? I don't want to leave the children, and Katie's still catching up on her sleep. Perhaps later we can go and explore the town.'

They did, at four in the afternoon when the worst of the heat had worn off. They walked down because the Jeeps were now one short, and the children skipped and scuffed up stones and seemed full of energy.

Gabby was too hot to skip, but she felt a bubbling excitement just the same. The noises and smells and sights were all strange and yet familiar from her very early childhood, and they saw things she'd forgotten.

On one street corner a man was grating ice over a huge plane, then packing the chips into a ball and covering it in hideously pink raspberry juice. He put it inside a folded cone of newspaper, then prepared another with condensed milk, grated coconut and chopped banana over the top.

'Gross,' Penny said with a shudder, but to Gabby, who was steaming gently in the tropical heat, it looked unbelievably inviting.

'The ice isn't safe, I suppose,' she said wistfully.

'Absolutely not. The water's probably straight out of the river. Come on, I want to go to the draper's and get some white cotton. I've run out.'

They went into a tiny shop, run by a wizened little Chinese woman with quick fingers and more wrinkles

than Gabby had ever seen, and then they came back
along the main street.

Penny indicated a sort of café, with people eating at
tables on the pavement. 'This is a *rumah makan*—literally a food house. It's our only restaurant, and the food's
brilliant. Indonesian and Chinese, and the kitchen's so
clean you can see your face in the counters, so we're
told. It's the only place to eat so it's just as well! We'll
take you one night. It's a real treat, and ridiculously
cheap.'

As they walked on Gabby was sure she could hear
the unmistakable roar of a football crowd. 'It's the satellite TV over the restaurant,' Penny explained. 'They
rent out space to watch it—the Indonesians are all foot-
ball-crazy, and they love the Australian and American
soaps. After the restaurant it's the town's most popular
venue!'

'Do they have *Children's BBC*?' Katie asked hopefully.

'Sorry, darling, no,' Penny told her oldest daughter.
'When we get electricity we can have a TV with a satellite dish, and you can watch cartoons—OK?'

'But we've got electricity,' Katie reasoned.

'But only a tiny generator and it's not big enough to
run a television. Sorry, darling.'

But it didn't pacify her. Katie trailed up the hill behind
them, scuffing her toes and looking mournful.

'Oh, dear. It's one of the adjustments she's going to
have to make,' Penny said. 'There's so much that's different. Still, the others managed to get used to it quite
quickly. I expect she will.'

They made their way slowly back to the bungalow
and were greeted by Rom with a brimming jug of freshly
made lemonade for the children and steaming tea for
the adults.

Gabby eyed the lemonade longingly but, as Penny assured her she would, she found the tea actually very refreshing.

Not so refreshing that she didn't very soon excuse herself and go back to bed until supper, and then escape again to return to her bed as early as she could decently do so.

It was worth it, though. She emerged the following morning after her *mandi* and early morning tea feeling refreshed and ready to start enjoying her holiday at last.

Jed was stretched out on the veranda, sipping fruit juice, with a little heap of papaya skins beside him on the table. She greeted him cheerfully, and he turned his head and looked up at her, without moving.

'Morning,' he said, and his voice sounded husky and interesting.

All that gin, Gabby thought. It probably wrecks the throat. She didn't dare look into those astonishingly blue eyes.

She helped herself to some fruit and sat down, nibbling as she looked out over the bay. It looked sparkling clear and inviting, and she longed to be out on it.

'We're going out in the launch today, I think,' he told her, as if he'd read her mind. 'There's nothing more we can do about the Jeep, and Derek's making some discreet enquiries about the other incidents. Until we find out what's wrong Jon thinks we should just carry on and not pay too much attention to it.'

'Do you agree?' she asked him, sensing that he was reluctant to criticise her cousin in front of her.

'I think he might be underestimating the situation,' he said carefully. 'I don't know what's wrong, but something's making them jumpy and someone's going to get badly hurt before long if this goes on.'

She remembered something her cousin had said the

night before last. 'Do you think it's just the Indonesians being targeted?' she asked.

There was a second's pause and then he shook his head. 'No. Anybody could have been driving that Jeep. Derek's wife could have been in the cookhouse—she's living up there with the others. She's an engineer too, and part of the team. They got married two months ago.'

'A female engineer? Doesn't that cause problems?'

He raised an eyebrow. 'Sexist?' he said softly.

She blushed. 'Not at all. I just thought, with all those men in the primitive conditions up there—well, bathrooms and that sort of thing—it's a bit difficult, I should think.'

'It's better now they've tied the knot. Indonesians can be a bit funny about women on their own. Married women, on the other hand, are quite safe. That was why I was a bit wary about you sharing the bungalow with me—I didn't want your reputation to suffer so that you lost respect.'

'My reputation matters to you?' she asked, feeling guilty for judging him so harshly last night but not at all convinced that he was genuinely concerned for her virtue and it wasn't just an excuse to get out of entertaining her.

'Well, perhaps not directly,' he said with a lazy grin. 'It might enhance mine, of course, which could be good news, but Jon's reputation could be affected and he needs to remain in a strong position to lead the team.' He stretched out his legs and propped them up on the veranda rail right in front of her eyes.

'As for the safety thing, I think we should all be vigilant. Jon's checking over the launch now, and making sure it hasn't been tampered with. The last thing we want is for it to break down and leave us adrift in the sea in the middle of the day in this heat.'

He eyed her bare arms critically. 'You'll need to cover up and smother yourself in sunblock,' he warned. 'And don't forget to take your anti-malarials.'

'Yes, Mummy,' she teased. 'Am I going to get this lecture every morning?'

He gave a wry grin. 'You can't be too careful. What pills are you taking?'

'Mefloquine—now you're going to tell me that's wrong.'

He laughed. 'I'm not—it's fine. It's the recommended drug. Just watch out for side-effects, but even they're better than dying of falciparum malaria.'

'What do you take?' she asked, somehow knowing it would be different.

He grinned. 'I'm trying a combination of other remedies.'

'What—marinading yourself in sweat and gin?' she said before she could stop herself.

To her relief he gave a short bark of laughter. 'Don't forget the tonic. The quinine in tonic was an early attempt to kill the malaria parasite spread by the *Anopheles* mosquito—you do know it's the female of the species that causes all the problems, typically?'

'Sexist?' she said softly, returning his little barb, and he grinned.

'Only mildly, and it is true. The female is the carrier of the parasite. Quinine was first used as an anti-malarial by the Indonesian folk doctors or *dukun*. Unfortunately this means it's been around for ages and so there's a lot of immunity to it now.'

'Hence the introduction of mefloquine.'

'Exactly. Chloroquine combined with proguanil, or alternatively doxycycline, causes fewer problems than mefloquine, but since none of them are especially desirable long term I'm trying to find out if anything else works any better—'

'Hence the gin and tonic.'

'Amongst other things.' He grinned. 'Hey, a man has to have some recreational activities, and what else do you see around here? Anyway, it's a good idea to take in plenty of fluids to replace the huge amount lost in sweat, and the juniper oil in gin acts as a natural insect repellent. Of course, rubbing yourself with a solution of tobacco juice is also effective—'

She wrinkled her nose. 'Nice,' she said with a grin. 'I could go off the tropics.'

He laughed again. 'There are hazards. The best thing to do is stay in the shade, cover up, use insect repellent and stay inside a screened area at dusk and during the night to avoid being bitten. The fluids are the easy bit. Want another drink?'

He was on his feet, heading for the kitchen, when Penny hailed them from down the road. 'We're off soon—are you ready?'

'Be with you in two shakes,' he called back. He looked at Gabby's arms and frowned. 'Cover up—have you got any long-sleeved shirts?'

'Only one clean one, and it's tight fitting and quite thick—and black.'

He rolled his eyes. 'Borrow one of my shirts. You can roll the sleeves up and tie the bottom, but it'll give you more protection. The sun shining off the sea will burn you in no time flat—and don't forget to put sunscreen on under your eyebrows and chin. Everybody gets sunburned there because they forget about reflections up from the water.'

'Mothering me again?' she said drily, heading for the kitchen with their plates.

He followed her. 'Just a little friendly medical advice.

I don't want to end up having to nurse you through malaria or heatstroke—and don't forget the hat.'

She rolled her eyes and he threw up his hands in mock surrender and backed out of the kitchen. 'OK, just don't say you weren't warned.'

She did cover up—in one of his shirts, freshly laundered and pressed to perfection, tied at the waist over loose cotton trousers and cotton tennis shoes.

'All right?' she asked, appearing outside her bedroom as he emerged from his.

He scanned her quickly, then those gloriously blue eyes locked with hers. 'Fine,' he said, and she wondered if it was her imagination or if he had sounded a bit curt.

He crammed the Panama hat down over his eyes so she couldn't really see them any more, and looked down at the bag in her hand. 'Got your swimming togs?'

'Of course—they're on, and I have spares. Now you're going to tell me I have to swim in a wetsuit because of jellyfish, and I'm probably going to hit you.'

'Oh, I love a bit of violence in a woman,' he teased, and pushed her gently out of the door. 'Come on, they'll be waiting.'

She was glad he couldn't see her face because the touch of his hand against her back had brought soft colour flooding to it. She had to fight the urge to lean back against him—and as much to escape from herself as from him—she hurried down the hill to where the others were now waiting.

'Where are we going?' she asked Penny as they drove down the road to the town. They were all squeezed into the Jeep, the children chattering excitedly beside them.

'A little island called Pulau Tengkorak—Monkey-Skull Island—so called because of the shape. It's fabulous—unpopulated except for a few monkeys and lizards, and of course the jellyfish, but they're mostly further out. Just keep your eyes open.'

She did, looking over the side of the launch into the sparkling clear water as they sliced through it on their way out to the island. She could see jellyfish, and flying fish jumping just yards from the launch, and she thought of the freezing fog and grey drizzle of England in November and forgave Indonesia its malaria mosquitoes. 'I can hardly wait to get in the water,' she told Penny. 'It looks so inviting.'

Penny nodded. 'It is. Warm and refreshing and wonderful, and of course there's plenty of shade from the palm trees. There are coconuts on the island—if any have fallen we can eat them with our lunch. The fresh ones are delicious, nothing like the dried-up remains that get into English supermarkets.' She pointed ahead of them. 'There it is.'

Gabby saw a little green dot growing on the horizon, and then within minutes they were there, pulling up near the beach and anchoring the launch to a buoy that floated in the surf.

'We have to wade the last few yards,' Penny told her. 'Keep your shoes on—in fact, keep them on the whole time, even for swimming. You never know what you might tread on.'

She climbed over the side into the knee-deep water, and found herself in Jed's warm and firm grip. 'OK?' he asked gruffly, before releasing her, and she could hardly function enough to nod in reply.

What was it about the man that every time he touched her she turned into an inferno? She shook her head slightly, scooped Katie up into her arms and carried her up the gently shelving slope to the shore. 'OK?' she asked her little travelling companion.

Katie nodded and grinned, quite happy to be carried

to the beach by the woman who had become her friend over the past few weeks. 'Yes, thanks,' she grinned. 'Are you going to swim with me?'

'I expect so. Shall we ask Mummy where we should put all our things?'

'They're up there,' she said, nodding up the beach to the edge of the treeline.

They walked up the sandy slope to the others, and Gabby wondered if she'd get away with spending all day with the children so she didn't have to spend any of it with Jed because she honestly thought she'd make a fool of herself if left to her own devices.

She wasn't to be that lucky. He appeared at her elbow with a bottle of factor 25 sunscreen, and ordered her to undress to her swimsuit.

'Even if you put your clothes back on it's a good idea,' he told her, and then stood waiting until she'd stripped off his shirt and her trousers and was standing in just a skimpy costume. Had she known he was going to do this she'd have worn the more modest one, but it was too late now. He turned her round, spread a dollop of cream over her neck and shoulders and smoothed it down her arms and back, then turned her round again, did her face and throat and down her chest until she pushed his hands away.

'I can manage now,' she told him firmly, and finished off the low neckline herself. Not for all the tea in China was he getting his fingertips down the neck of her costume!

He handed her the bottle. 'Return the favour?' he asked, and, as if it hadn't been bad enough to have him touching her, she now had to run her hands over acres of bronzed Hollywood potential. 'I'll do your back,' she muttered, and went round behind him.

She was a little on the rough side in self-defence, but

it was either that or linger longingly on the supple, satiny skin that her fingers itched to explore. She finished off with a last defiant swipe, squirted enough into her hand to do her legs and handed the bottle back to him.

'Thanks,' he said, and she could have sworn his voice was a little gruff.

Him too, eh? That could make life interesting. Too interesting. She wasn't into holiday romances, and she had no doubts about Jed. He was a love 'em and leave 'em man if ever she'd met one, and there was no way he was loving and leaving *her*.

She slapped on the last of the sun cream, helped Penny spread some on the children and then went to explore the sea.

She was just about to dive into the gently rippling surf when a hand clamped on her shoulder, making her jump. 'Mind—there's a jellyfish beside you.'

She looked down to where Jed pointed, and saw a soft, pale parachute, undulating gently in the water. Almost invisible, it was beautiful to watch.

'Are they dangerous?' she asked, fascinated by the slow movement.

'Not those. They sting a bit—and they sting where they're washed up on the beach, too, so be careful where you walk. You should also keep an eye out for rocks under the sand and avoid them. This beach is fine, but others have stonefish and sea urchins, and they're deadly, quite literally. Remember to keep your shoes on and your eyes open.'

He drew her to the side. 'Here, I've checked this bit. Just wallow. It's wonderful.'

She sank down under the water, revelling in its gentle caress, and sighed with delight. 'Oh, it's glorious.'

'Glad you came?' he asked softly.

'Oh, yes.'

'Despite the malaria and the flukes and the leeches and the hepatitis and the rabies and the filariasis and—'

'Yes!' she said with a laugh. 'Even so! Are you trying to put me off?'

He grinned, his head floating above the water just inches from hers. 'Would I?'

'Probably,' she said drily.

'Oh, I don't know. I'm beginning to think having you over here for a holiday may not be all bad after all. If all else fails, you can always help me with the sick list.'

'What sick list?' she scoffed. 'You don't have a sick list. You ship them all off to Jakarta!'

He grinned. 'Rumbled. Ah, well. You can help me with my malaria research—'

She chucked a handful of water in his face and swam away from him, laughing. She thought she'd got away with it until she felt long, strong fingers close around her ankle and jerk her backwards. She shot through the water and cannoned into him, and the sudden contrast of coarse hair against her back and legs did nothing for her composure.

He stood up, drawing her to her feet, and turned her into his arms. 'Forfeit,' he said softly, and then before she could move his lips were on hers and her mouth was opening to him. Heat flooded her, and with a little moan she leant into him and felt the solid pressure of his response.

That nearly finished her. With a little cry she pushed him away, and turned and swam back to the others, wondering if they'd seen and if so what they'd make of it.

They were all engrossed in a game of water polo, and she went and joined in. Jed, she noticed out of the corner of her eye, went up the beach to their bags, took out a towel and lay down in the shade with his hat over his eyes.

Good. She didn't need any more challenges to her nervous system like that one. She was beginning to think that in terms of mortal danger malaria was the least of her worries!

CHAPTER THREE

THEY stayed all day on the tiny island, playing in the water until it was too hot, then lurking in the shade at the fringe of the palm trees and eating the picnic that Rom had prepared for them.

There were little sticks of spicy chicken satay with a tasty peanut sauce, cold roasted chicken legs, avocados and, of course, lots of fresh fruit and plenty to drink. Jed wandered off and came back with a couple of fresh, young coconuts, and with a vicious-looking knife called a *parang* he laid about the green husks, poked out the three eyes in the top of each nut and poured the sweet, translucent coconut milk into a jug.

Then he hacked the coconuts into chunks and handed them out, and they used their teeth to scrape off the tender white flesh from the hard shell. Gabby couldn't believe the flavour.

'Good?' Penny asked with a smile.

'Amazing—it's nothing like the ones you can buy in supermarkets in England!'

'Told you. You'll be spoilt now—you'll have to keep coming back.'

Gabby stretched out on her towel and sighed. 'It could certainly be addictive,' she agreed. 'Just think, back home it's cold and rainy—foul!' She wriggled a little on the towel, rearranging the soft sand under her back to conform better to her contours, and shut her eyes.

The conversation droned quietly around her, and she lay completely relaxed and tried to follow the words, but it was too much like hard work. Perhaps she'd just lie there…

The next thing she knew was a tickling sensation around her ribs. Her eyes flew open and she lifted her head to find Jed, sitting next to her dribbling fine sand over her midriff. There were little piles of it all over her costume, tiny slithering pyramids that ran together when she moved.

His smile had a slightly alarming quality, rather like the smile of a tiger. There was no sign of the others, she noted with a little shiver of panic as she looked around.

'They've gone for a wander round the island,' he told her, as if he'd read her mind, and made another pyramid on her stomach. 'I volunteered to babysit.' His teasing grin did silly things to her, and her memory would keep re-running the kiss, which did her no good at all.

'Why do I need to be sat on?' she asked a little breathlessly, watching the sand. 'I'm hardly going to get into mischief.'

'Snakes,' he said calmly. 'They come down out of the jungle and curl up on you when you're sleeping—I had to guard you.'

She gave him a sceptical look. 'You, guard me?' She snorted softly. 'You're joking, of course.'

He grinned that devastating grin of his. 'Of course— there aren't any snakes that dangerous on the island, but it was worth a try just to get you looking adoringly at me as your saviour.'

'I didn't,' she said dampeningly.

The grin widened. 'No—great shame. Still, I'll keep trying. Want a drink?'

She sat up, spilling sand all over her legs. 'Yes, please. What is there?'

'Beer, lemonade, coconut milk, fruit juice.'

She opted for lemonade as the safest choice. She'd

had a great deal of fruit already, and until her system adjusted she didn't want to push her luck.

It was freshly made, cold and sharp and gorgeous. He was pretty gorgeous, too, she had to admit. He was wearing his shirt open over his swimming trunks, and the little glimpses she had of his chest were almost more enticing than the lemonade.

'Fancy a stroll?' he suggested, and she dragged her mind back under control.

'Around the island? Is it far?'

He didn't answer because Jon came running back just at that moment, carrying little Tom who was screaming and thrashing in his arms.

'Uh-oh. Looks like he's been stung by something,' Jed said, getting to his feet. 'Problems?' he called, sprinting towards them.

'Jellyfish—he stood right in the middle of one on the beach. I told him not to, but he didn't realise it would squelch over the top of his shoes.'

They came back to Gabby, Jed examining Tom's foot as they hurried over the sand. 'Any idea what sort?' Jed asked, rummaging in a bag.

'Not really—big pink job.'

He nodded and, taking off the shoe, held Tom's foot firmly in a bowl and sloshed something dark brown over it.

'What's that?' Gabby asked, peering over his shoulder and sniffing.

'Vinegar—it's the cheapest and most effective remedy. That and meat tenderiser paste—don't ask me why, I haven't got a clue, but it really takes the sting out. It's brilliant for Portuguese man-of-war stings, too.'

'Whatever happened to good old-fashioned antihistamine cream?' Gabby said wryly.

'It's a bit low-key for some of these things. I do use

conventional antihistamines and adrenaline in case of emergency and anaphylactic shock, and I always carry it with me wherever I go just to be on the safe side, but for this sort of thing cooking ingredients seem to have it licked. Right, Tom, my old son, how does that feel now?'

'Better,' the boy said with a sorrowful sniff. 'It hurt vewwy badly.'

Jed ruffled the boy's hair and stood up. 'Where are the girls?' he asked, searching the beach.

'Probably looking for us. I didn't have time to let them know what was happening, I just picked him up and ran. I don't suppose you'd like to go and find them? They were just near that rocky outcrop when we saw them last.'

Jed screwed the lid on the vinegar and turned to Gabby. 'Fancy that stroll now?' he asked.

Alone? With him?

'I dare you,' he said softly, so softly that Jon and Tom didn't hear over the little boy's sniffling.

Their eyes locked. 'Really daring,' she murmured somewhat scathingly, and pretended that her heart wasn't thumping at the thought of being alone with him. Nevertheless, she got to her feet, brushed the sand off her legs and put her shoes back on.

Murphy's law being what it was, she lost her balance and swayed against him, and felt the hard thrust of his thigh against her hip. By the time she'd straightened up she'd coloured beautifully and, being the gentleman he was, he grinned knowingly at her and made the situation worse.

She stepped well away from him, looked back over her shoulder and tipped her chin up a touch. 'Well? Are you coming?'

He bent over Tom. 'All right now, little man?'

Tom nodded, and Jed straightened, picking up a bottle of the lemonade and dangling it from his fingers. 'Let's go, then.'

She put his shirt on again to protect herself from the sun, then fell into step, although not quite beside him. She maintained a careful distance between them, but if she thought she'd got away with it, without him noticing, she was wrong.

'I don't bite,' he said mildly, strolling some ten feet away from her. 'You'll be walking in the water to get away from me soon, and you shouldn't be in the sun anyway. Come back here in the shade and stop behaving like a Victorian virgin. I promise you, I'm quite harmless.'

She snorted. Jed, harmless? And she was a monkey's uncle!

He did behave, though, after she came back in the shade, and then she had to deal with an emotion that felt suspiciously like disappointment.

It didn't last long. Gabby was too busy enjoying the strange vegetation and the sparkling clear blue sea and the cloudless sky—except that it wasn't cloudless. Rainclouds were building fast over Pulau Panjang and heading towards them, and she got the distinct feeling it was about to rain very, very heavily—

'We're going to get caught in that,' Jed said as she thought it, and, taking her hand, he led her at a run along the beach to the place Jon had mentioned where the rocks stuck out into the sea. There was a big outcrop with an overhang, and clustered underneath it they saw Penny and the girls.

'Hi,' she called. 'Have you seen Jon and Tom?'

'Back at base camp—Tom's trodden in a jellyfish,' Jed told her. 'It didn't seem too bad—I've dealt with it.

They sent us to tell you where they are and make sure you were all right.'

'We're fine. We've been puddling about in rock pools, haven't we, girls?'

The girls nodded excitedly and began to tell them about all the funny things they'd seen.

'You didn't put your hands or feet into the water, did you?' Jed warned.

Penny shook her head. 'No. We know about nasties that live in rock pools. Anyway, we looked up and saw the sky, and came in here to shelter from the rain when it comes.'

'Which is now,' Jed said with a laugh, and pulled Gabby down and under the shelter of the rock just as the rain swept up the beach from the sea and flung itself against the little island. Once again she was amazed at the torrential streams that fell, blocking out their view of the sea and turning the beach to a river.

They played games and told stories to keep the children's minds off the storm, but it was short-lived. It stopped after about half an hour, and they crawled out from under their rocky umbrella into glorious sunshine.

'Look, a rainbow!' Daisy said excitedly, and pointed at the horizon.

'Oh, Mummy, wow!' Katie breathed.

Gabby could have echoed her. There was a perfect arch spanning the sky, the colours more radiant and glorious than she had ever seen. She stared at it, spellbound, for endless seconds, before sighing and turning to Penny. 'Why is it that the colours here are brighter and more— more *coloured* than they are at home?'

Penny laughed. 'I suppose they are—I don't know why. It must be something to do with the light.'

'Perhaps you're just more relaxed?' Jed suggested.

Relaxed? With him two feet away?

'I think it must be something to do with the angle of the sun,' Gabby said, ignoring his suggestion.

'Possibly. Come on, girls, let's go back to Daddy and let Jed and Gabby get on with their walk,' Penny said to the children, and herded them gently back in the direction of the boat, ignoring Katie's protests.

Jed turned to Gabby. 'Want to carry on round? It'll take about half an hour.'

'What about Tom's foot?'

Jed shrugged. 'It was a simple sting. He'll be fine. Anyway, I want to talk to you. I've got a proposition to put to you.'

Gabby's eyes widened and she backed up slightly, making his lips quirk.

'Don't jump to conclusions,' he teased. 'Come on, let's walk and talk.'

They walked, but for a long time they didn't talk—or at least not about what Jed wanted to discuss. Gabby was so busy being fascinated that she wasn't really paying attention, and he didn't seem to be in a tearing hurry to broach whatever subject he had in mind.

Perhaps, she thought with mild curiosity, he was biding his time—or perhaps it had just been an excuse to get her alone on the other side of the island, away from the others.

And do what? she scoffed at herself. Seduce her?

She was being ridiculous. Whatever else he was, he was easygoing and good-natured. If seduction was in his mind and she said no, he'd accept it, she was sure. She was less sure that she'd say no, and that worried her just a touch. Maybe he knew that, too? Even more worrying!

She managed to convince herself that he didn't want to talk to her at all but just wanted to get her alone, and so she continued to plague him with questions about the trees and undergrowth and the composition of the sand, which was smooth and tracked with rivulets after the downpour—anything rather than silence.

Not that there was much of that, either. Lizards scuttled about, birds flashed overhead and she saw and heard monkeys screeching in the trees and swinging from branch to branch with casual ease. Every now and then one would stop for a moment and watch them with bright, intelligent eyes.

'I wonder what they think of us?' she murmured, returning the level stare of a young male.

'Not a lot, if they've got any sense. We either ruin their habitat or eat them, depending on how civilised our culture is. Either way, I don't suppose they're exactly grateful.'

Gabby laughed softly. 'If you put it like that, I suppose you're probably right. I wonder if they can philosophise?'

He rolled his eyes and carried on walking, and she fell into step beside him again and wondered when he was going to make his move.

She didn't have to wait long. Apparently the time was right because he turned to her and tipped his head towards the trunk of a fallen tree. 'Come and sit down,' he suggested, and made himself comfortable on the trunk. He uncapped the bottle of lemonade and handed it to her.

Warily, she sat a discreet distance away from him and took a swig, then handed it back and waited.

He drank deeply, recapped the bottle and put it down. 'Do you like it out here?' he asked after a second or two.

'On this island?' she asked, surprised. This was not what she'd expected.

'Pulau Panjang.'

She shrugged. 'It's only been three days. I suppose

it's all right. The scenery's gorgeous, the town's colourful and noisy and smelly, and the people seem
friendly enough if you discount the trouble up at the
power station compound—why?'

He shrugged and grinned at her. 'I was just wondering. I heard you talking to Penny about not having a job
so there's no need for you to rush back, I imagine, unless
there's some significant other you haven't told me
about?'

'No significant other.' Or insignificant, come to that,
she thought with an internal sigh. Nobody that cared or
mattered at all, depressing though it was. 'Why?'

He shrugged again. 'I could do with a research assistant,' he told her with a lazy smile.

'Research assistant?' she exclaimed, staring at him in
amazement. 'What on earth for?'

'My anti-malarial research project, of course,' he said
as if it was obvious. He was totally deadpan, and she
thought again what a loss he was to the film industry—
or poker.

Research project indeed, she thought, and laughed.
'You must be joking! You seriously imagine you can
persuade me to stay out here and join you on that veranda, sousing myself in gin and tonic and watching the
world go by while I wait to get malaria? Get real, Jed!
Life's too short to spend playing Hollywood bit-parts to
the natives.'

'There is rather more to it than that,' he said mildly,
but she didn't let him finish because the light had
dawned and she suddenly realised exactly what he was
suggesting. Yes, his aim had been seduction, only not
now but later, longer term and pre-arranged. Rather more
to it, indeed! She hung onto her temper with difficulty.

'No, thank you,' she said firmly.

'Sure I can't persuade you? The terms and conditions are very flexible,' he said with a grin.

'I'll bet.' She gave a huffy sigh. 'Look, Jed, I'm not in the market for an affair. I want a real job, thank you, not some thinly disguised excuse to get me into bed. Find a nice little native girl to cuddle up to if you're lonely at night, but leave me out of it. I'm sorry, I'm not buying. You don't interest me.'

He stared at her in stunned amazement. 'My God, you're arrogant,' he murmured.

She exploded. 'Me, arrogant? Just where the hell do you get off calling *me* arrogant? You have the infernal nerve to suggest setting up some cosy little love nest in the name of your bogus research—research, for heaven's sake! What research? You're such a fraud, Jed Daniels— and, for the record, you leave me cold.'

She stalked off but he followed her, grasped her arm and turned her back, pulling her hard up against his chest.

'Liar,' he said softly. His eyes glittered dangerously, and she wondered what she'd done, angering him when they were so far from the others. After all, what did she really know of him?

'I am not,' she protested, pushing feebly against his rock-hard chest. It didn't budge an inch. 'Idle lounge-lizards are not at all my type,' she added, just to ram the point home.

'Is that why you kissed me back this morning?' he murmured just inches from her mouth.

'I didn't,' she protested, but he cut off her argument by the simple expedient of sealing his lips over hers and stifling the words. His mouth was firm and yet soft, and after a few moments it softened further, coaxing, sipping and teasing, and she felt her resistance ebbing away.

She was powerless to resist the probe of his tongue,

and her mouth opened to him, giving him what he so gently demanded. She felt the silken stroke of his tongue over hers, hot and salty with a faint trace of lemon from the drink they'd shared, and then her body exploded into molten heat and she sagged against him with a little cry.

He might have been a gentleman, but he wasn't a saint. He took only what she offered, and when his large, hot palm closed over her breast she gasped and leant on him even harder. His other hand cupped her bottom and lifted her hard against him, and the tattered remains of her mind seemed to flutter to the sand at their feet.

'Yes,' he sighed against her throat as she trailed her tongue over his jaw. Her fingertips threaded through the hair on his chest, seeking the hot, damp skin beneath. Everything was hot, she thought vaguely. Hot and humid and torrid and a little like a dream, not quite connected to reality. What on earth was she doing?

His fingers were kneading her breast and her head felt too heavy. It fell back, and she felt the heat of his mouth on the vulnerable slope of her throat. There was a gentle suck, and a nip, then the soothing sweep of his tongue over the tender skin.

It nearly drove her wild. She felt herself clawing at his clothes, pushing the open shirt off his shoulders, whimpering slightly as the fabric resisted, and then suddenly he was releasing her and stepping back.

She nearly fell at his feet.

'Now tell me you're not interested,' he said dangerously softly, and, turning on his heel, he walked ahead, leaving her standing there rooted to the spot.

'Damn you, Jed,' she muttered under her breath. 'Damn you to hell and back—*I am not interested*!' she yelled after him.

She trudged after him through the soft, thick sand that sucked at her feet and made her calves ache. She didn't dare take her eyes off the ground she was walking on unless she trod on a snake or lizard. Beside her the monkeys screeched and ripped through the trees with ridiculous ease, and she wished she could do that. At least she wouldn't have to walk through the sand!

It probably only took about ten minutes to get back to the others, but it seemed more like hours. She was hot, she was tired and she was ready to kill. She was also embarrassed at herself.

Penny shot her a searching look but she avoided the other woman's eyes and wouldn't be drawn. 'How's Tom's foot?' she asked, exhibiting a professional interest.

'Oh, Jed's dealt with it—it's fine. It's so reassuring having him around.'

She heard a soft snort from the man in question, but she didn't look at him either. They were packing up to go home, and she helped with the loading of the bags onto the boat and the ferrying of the children.

Once on the launch she found herself a nice secluded spot in front of the wheelhouse, well away from Jed and Penny and the children, and sat under her hat, enjoying the cool breeze as they chugged across the stretch of water to Telok Panjang.

The water was magical. As they were approaching the town the sun was low in the sky, and the phosphorescence in the water was wonderful. She imagined at night it would be stunning, the sparkling green trails left by the flying fish and the wake of the boat quite spectacular.

It would be wonderfully romantic to share it with a lover, she thought in a moment of weakness, and then remembered Jed and his proposition. Maybe she ought to stop being such a prude and take him up on it?

Although she was by no means the Victorian virgin he'd accused her of being, she was very far from liberal in her morals. Perhaps it was time to make a change, she thought, and then remembered that she'd rather burned her boats in that department.

And they had to go back to the bungalow and live together for the next three weeks! She groaned inwardly, wondering how she could have put him down without being quite so forceful so that they were both left with a shred of dignity instead of the awkward and uneasy silence that had existed between them ever since their 'talk'.

Penny came and sat beside her and smiled a little warily. 'OK?' she asked.

'Fine. It's beautiful up here, I'm enjoying the view.'

'Good. Um—look, Gabby, is everything all right with you and Jed?'

She stared at the island, feigning interest. 'Of course. Why wouldn't it be?'

'I just wondered,' the other woman said softly. 'Only Jed seems a bit crusty and irritable, which isn't like him at all. He's normally so easygoing. I just wondered if anything happened on your walk—but it's none of my business. Ignore me.'

'Good heavens,' Gabby said with a false little laugh. 'Whatever could have happened on our walk? Penny, relax, everything's fine.'

And the moon was made of cheese.

Oh, hell.

As they drew near the jetty they could see a cluster of people, waving and shouting, and Jed came round beside the wheelhouse and held his hand above his eyes, peering at the crowd. His mouth was tight, and Gabby looked away. Was he still mad with her? Or was he worried?

She looked at the jetty and saw people were gesticulating at them to hurry.

'Something's wrong,' Jed murmured, squinting at the crowd. 'What the hell's happened now?'

Penny came up beside her and joined the inspection. 'Oh, no. Whatever can it be?'

They scrambled to their feet and headed back to the well of the boat, ready to disembark as soon as possible, and as they drew up alongside the jetty she saw Rom, the pretty young Indonesian servant who worked for Jon and Penny, weeping and calling out to Penny.

There was also a crowd of men in uniforms, and as they tied up and climbed out of the boat, one of the men with more gold braid than the others stepped forward, his eyes flicking from Jed to Jon.

'Tuan Andrews?'

'That's me,' Jonathan said. 'What's the matter?'

The man looked unhappy. 'We have a situation,' he said in stilted English. 'Some of your engineers—they seem to have been captured by men from the hill tribe.'

Gabby felt the blood drain from her face.

'Captured?' Jon said in a shocked voice. 'Who?'

'Tuan and Ibu Beckers, Ismail Barrung, Jumani Tandak and Luther Tarupadang.'

'Derek and Sue,' Penny said with a wail. 'But Sue's pregnant!'

'Sorry, mem,' the chief of police said to her. 'It's a bad business. Very bad.'

'Mummy, what's happened?' Katie was asking. 'What's wrong?'

'Nothing, darling,' she assured her, and gathered the children close. 'Nothing at all.'

But her eyes were wide with fear, and Gabby knew this was what she'd been dreading for two days. It was no longer just the Indonesians. They could no longer pretend.

All of them were in danger.

CHAPTER FOUR

'I WANT you to leave the island.'

Jonathan's voice was rough with worry, but Penny was implacable.

'I'm not leaving you,' she said firmly. 'I think we should all go. It clearly isn't safe—'

'I can't leave,' Jonathan said just as firmly. 'I have to stay here and get to the bottom of this. The engineers' lives could depend on it.'

'Your life could depend on you getting away,' Penny replied, and they could tell the strain was getting to her by the shake in her voice. Jed shook his head and looked across at Gabby, sitting with him on the veranda just outside the bedroom where Jon and Penny were having their argument.

'Do you think we should all leave?' Gabby asked softly.

Jed shrugged. 'Who knows? Until the chief of police comes and we find out more about what happened, I don't think we can tell, but I have to say I'm not concerned about the children. Indonesians dote on children, they wouldn't hurt them. Children are sacred, whatever their parents may have done.'

'You seem very sure.'

His smile flashed white in the darkness. 'I am sure. They're quite safe. Jonathan is probably most at risk of the five of them.'

'What about you?'

'Me?' He sounded surprised. 'I'm not at risk—I'm just the doctor, I'm not really anything to do with the project.' He tipped back his chair, propped his feet on the rail and stared out over the dark sea. A boat carved a gleaming, greenish wake in the phosphorescence, and here and there lights twinkled.

Behind them she could hear Penny weeping quietly, and her cousin's gentle reassurance.

Gabby's mind stayed locked on their problem. 'Will the developer come out to see what's going on?' she asked.

'Bill Freeman?' Jed shrugged again. 'Maybe. He's been quite involved up to now. It depends what the problem is, but I don't think Jon's told him about the sabotage attempts yet.'

The lights of a vehicle appeared on the track up from the town, and the battered old police car spluttered to a halt near the veranda.

Jed unfolded himself from his chair and ambled down the steps to greet the police chief, while Gabby went in to tell Jonathan of his arrival.

'Stay with Penny, she's upset,' her cousin pleaded, and so she went in to the other woman and comforted her. Outside on the veranda they could hear the murmured conversation of the three men, and then the sound of a vehicle clattering to life signalled the end of the police visit.

Jonathan came in again and sat heavily on the end of the bed. 'No news. They still don't know why it's happened, but they're sending an officer up to the next village to find out what he can. They expect him back by tomorrow night, and in the meantime they've left an armed guard to protect us, just as a precaution.'

Penny's eyes widened. 'Armed?' she whispered.

'Just to be on the safe side—he's not convinced it's necessary. I had to talk him into leaving the man at all.'

Gabby eyed her cousin thoughtfully. He was lying,

she could tell. Was the situation worse than they'd been told at first?

'Excuse me, I think I'll go back to the bungalow now,' she said to them, and slipped out. Jed was on the veranda, as she'd expected, and she beckoned him.

He stood and followed her up the track. Out of the corner of her eye she could see the guard, lolling against a tree, and she could smell the sweet, heavy scent of the clove tobacco he was smoking. He didn't look much of a deterrent to determined and desperate men, Gabby thought with a little shiver of nerves.

'What did he say?' she asked once they were out of earshot.

'They came at two in the afternoon when the men were resting. They always lie down for a while after lunch and start work again after the rain when it's a bit cooler. They came while they were asleep, and took them.'

'How?' Gabby asked. 'Surely the road doesn't go very far.'

'They were on foot, so had the alarm been raised quickly it might have been possible to catch up with them, but by the time the cook-boy got back from town at five they were long gone and the trail had been destroyed by the rain.'

'So how do they know when they were taken?'

'A note from Derek, apparently dictated by the captors and translated by one of the engineers.' He stopped, obviously reluctant to say any more, but Gabby pressed him.

'What did it say apart from that?'

Jed sighed quietly. 'Just a threat to kill them if the project proceeds.'

'Oh, my God.'

'Quite. These boys aren't messing around, they mean business.'

He looked at his watch. 'Fancy dinner?'

'But Rom isn't up to cooking—wasn't her husband one of the engineers who was captured? I thought Penny had given her the night off so she could go home to her family?'

'I meant in town, at the *rumah makan*.'

She stared at him in amazement. 'They could be killed and you want to go out for dinner?' she exclaimed, her voice rising. 'Anyway, I thought you didn't entertain tourists.'

He gave her a level look. 'I don't, but I still have to eat. Anyway, before you get carried away about why I want your company, I want to go down to town and sound out a few people I know, but I don't want to leave you here on your own and I think Jon and Penny could do with a little privacy right now.'

'I'd be all right on my own—'

'No, and, anyway, you have to eat as well. We'll go to the *rumah makan* and have a meal, and then wander through the town as if I'm giving you a guided tour. We'll be quite safe, but I can casually make a few enquiries while we're down there.'

'More people who owe you favours?' she asked with a thread of sarcasm. The last thing she felt like doing was going out for a meal to celebrate. 'What did you do, save their children's lives?'

'Actually, yes.'

Colour scorched her cheeks and she was suddenly ashamed of her suspicious mind. 'Sorry. That was un-called-for. Yes, of course I'll come.'

They set off in the Jeep, after telling the others where they were going, and Gabby discovered to her surprise that she was actually starving. While they were waiting for the food to be put in front of them they sat at a table on the street outside amongst the other customers and the smoking mosquito coils, and while her stomach grumbled quietly to itself Gabby marvelled at the way Jed networked the locals.

'Nobody wants to talk,' he confided under his breath at one point. 'They all know more than they're saying, but they're keeping out of it.'

The food arrived then, great heaps of *nasi goreng* or fried rice, with *satay* and dried salt fish and curry and sweet and sour chicken and innumerable other side dishes, all spicy and tasty and quite delicious.

'Save some room,' Jed warned as she piled in, eating—as he did—with her fingers, balling the rice into neat pellets with her right hand and popping them into her mouth. It was, in fact, an easy way to eat once she'd mastered the art of making the grains of rice stick together, but again there was the question of the right and left hand—the right for eating and greeting, the left for toilet purposes.

So much to remember, she thought as she ate yet another strip of the salty dried fish.

'Why do I need to save room?' she mumbled around the tasty fragments.

'Because we're going visiting, and the Indonesians are such hospitable people they just have to feed visitors.'

Gabby groaned, thinking of the vast amount she'd just put away. 'You might have warned me sooner!'

'You'll cope.' He caught the waiter's eye, haggled for a moment over the bill and then paid up once honour was satisfied on both sides. They took the Jeep and drove down to the harbour, then parked it and wandered along the seafront.

The town was slightly L-shaped, wrapped around the mouth of the river on one side. On the other side was a small *kampung*, or village, a much poorer community altogether. It was to there they were headed, she discovered.

Jed hailed a water-taxi, a rickety little boat with a hissing kerosene lantern, hanging from a bamboo pole, and an outboard that had seen better days. It spluttered to life once they were seated, and the boat chugged across the estuary to the little settlement on the other side. Jed asked the boatman to wait, and then handed Gabby ashore and ushered her along the jetty, a makeshift raft linked to the wooden walkways that stretched out over the water like fingers.

Between them were simple houses, lit with the yellow glow of kerosene, all family life taking place behind the open doorways. 'They don't go much on privacy, do they?' Gabby murmured.

'Only for certain things. Men and women never touch each other in public except in a very asexual way, and they never hold hands or kiss like we do in the west, but they have much more contact between people of the same sex. Indonesians are great touchers and huggers.'

He turned left and right and left, and then finally stopped outside a sorry little shack with a thin, tired-looking woman sitting on the step nursing a baby.

Jed crouched down and greeted her, and she scrambled to her feet and ran inside, calling to the others and beckoning the visitors in.

'Take off your shoes—and don't touch the children's heads,' Jed muttered, and then they were inside the little room and being greeted by all the family.

There was the now familiar smell of mosquito coils smouldering quietly near the doorway to deter the worst of the villains, and also the sweet, cloying scent of the clove cigarettes that were so popular. Drinks were brought out—the incredibly strong and sickly sweet coffee she'd learnt to avoid—and tiny cakes, nuts and other delicacies were spread out in front of them on the floor. Although she couldn't understand a word, the women kept giving her sidelong glances and giggling behind their hands.

'Do they think we're an item?' she asked Jed in a lull, and he laughed.

'Probably. You might be kind and play along with it—I've been religiously celibate and they think there's something wrong with me.'

She chuckled. Jed, celibate? Surely there was no need. The young women were looking at him as if they could eat him, and at least two of them were nursing babies!

Finally, after all the social niceties had been satisfied and Gabby had eaten more sickly little cakes than she thought she could keep down, Jed and Jamal, the head of the house, seemed to turn their talk to other things. They went into a huddle in the corner, and Gabby suddenly found herself the centre of attention.

The young women touched her clothes and smiled shyly, and one fingered her hair, marvelling at the colour and texture, so unlike their own. A baby crept onto her lap and tugged at a curl, and she laughed and hugged it, just stopping herself from kissing its head.

It used her as a climbing frame, pulling itself up and bouncing on her lap just like her nieces and nephews did, and she held onto the chubby little brown arms and let it bounce, laughing when it sat down with a plonk.

She looked up then to find the other children clustered round her, all reaching out to touch her hair. They didn't seem to have the same inhibitions as the adults about touching heads, and as she had none at all she sat there and let them maul her gently.

A hand on her shoulder made her turn her head, and

she looked round to find Jed standing behind her, an enigmatic look on his face.

'Time to go?' she asked wistfully.

'If you can tear yourself away.'

She stood up, and one of the young women went out the back and returned with a length of batik cloth, beautifully dyed in the most wonderful jewel colours, and pressed it into Gabby's hands.

She turned to Jed. 'It's lovely—why's she showing it to me? Did she make it?'

'It's a gift,' Jed told her. 'A sarong.'

'A gift? Oh, but I couldn't possibly accept!' she protested, stunned by the girl's generosity.

'You have to. They'd be desperately insulted if you refused it.'

'Really? Could I offer to pay for it?'

He shook his head. 'Absolutely not. Just take it, Gabby.'

She turned back to the girl, unbearably touched, and hugged her. 'Thank you,' she said simply, blinking away the tears that filled her eyes, and all the women hugged her and patted her and sent her on her way with a warm glow she hadn't felt in years.

She clutched the cloth against her chest all the way home, amazed that she should have been made such a gift.

She stroked the fabric, and found it was fine and soft and felt quite wonderful against her skin. 'Why did they give it to me?' she asked Jed as they climbed the road out of the town.

'The man with the pneumothorax is her intended— you helped to save his life. They've heard you're a healer, and your unusual colouring backs that up.' He shrugged and grinned. 'Seems like they just wanted to say thank you.'

'I wonder where they got the idea from that I'm a healer?' she murmured drily, still stroking the cloth.

He laughed and pulled the Jeep to a halt outside her cousin's bungalow. Lights were burning brightly in the sitting room, spilling out across the veranda. 'They're still up—let's go and tell them what we've found out,' Jed suggested.

The security guard was asleep under a tree and jumped as they approached. Jed spoke to him in rapid Indonesian and he struggled to his feet and straightened his uniform, grinning sheepishly.

'Useless,' Jed growled. 'They just aren't taking this seriously, but they'd better.'

Gabby shot him a keen look in the dim light from the windows. 'Why? You still haven't told me what you found out. Why do we need to take this so seriously?'

'Because they mean business. Come on.'

He pushed open the screen door and went in, to find Jonathan and Penny sitting together on the sofa. Penny had been crying, and Jon looked distracted and tired. They both jumped up as Jed and Gabby went in.

'You're back—thank God,' Penny said, looking relieved. 'I was worried about you.'

'There's no need,' Jed assured her. He folded himself into a chair, crossed one leg over the other and sighed, dropping his head back against the cushions.

'Well? Did you find anything out?' Jon asked urgently, clearly irritated by his casual attitude and impatient to hear the news.

'Oh, yes. Jamal wouldn't tell me why they want us to stop, but these hill people apparently are quite fierce and have powerful magic.'

'Magic? I thought this lot were Christians?' Jon said, looking confused.

'They are—after a fashion. Indonesian beliefs are all

a little tangled. Anyway, everyone's a little afraid of this lot, although they very rarely venture down to the town. They're hunter-gatherers in the main, rather like the Dyaks, and their religion is largely animist with the odd fragment of Christianity.'

'Are the two compatible?'

Jed laughed softly. 'In Indonesia almost all religions are compatible, and if they aren't they alter them until they fit. Whatever, these people could be dangerous, and they mean to stop us building the dam. What we don't know is why, but you can bet your life it's tied up in *adat*.'

'*Adat*?' Gabby repeated. 'What's that?'

'Custom, tradition, social order and behaviour patterns, ways that things are done or not done. There's a tremendous amount of ceremonial attached to all their religious practices, whatever the religion. What we need to do is find out whose toes we're treading on and why, and then we might stand a chance of negotiating a settlement.'

'Did Jamal think—? Are they—? Oh, Lord, Jed, they will be all right, won't they? I can't bear to think of Sue pregnant and going through all this.'

'I'm more worried about Derek and his diabetes. If he didn't take insulin with him he could be in trouble already,' Jed told them.

'Bill phoned—he's arriving tomorrow afternoon. He's bringing his plane so you can overfly the site and get a closer look, see if that sheds any light.'

'We might also see if we can spot any woodsmoke or signs of habitation further up—give us an idea of where to start looking.' Jed jackknifed out of the chair and looked at Gabby. 'Time for bed, I think. Tomorrow could be a very long day.'

She nodded and stood up, following him out past the dozing security guard.

'That man's a waste of space,' Jed muttered as they went into the bungalow. 'I think it might be a good idea to sleep together tonight.'

Gabby shot him a look. 'Excuse me?'

'Relax, I have no designs on your virtue. Actually, I think it's probably me taking the risk, but I'll tough it out if you promise to be gentle with me.'

She had to laugh. It was that or scream. 'Do as you wish. I shall be in my room, in my bed, alone. Where you choose to sleep is up to you.'

She went into her room, undressed and wrapped herself in a towel and went out to the *mandi*. When she came back it was to find Jed sprawled on another bed apparently dragged in from his room, wearing nothing but a sarong fastened round his waist.

She raised an eyebrow witheringly—she hoped. It didn't wither him. He smirked, vaulted off the bed and snagged his towel on the way out of the door. 'Yell if you need me,' he said with a grin.

'In your dreams,' she muttered under her breath, and he laughed and shut the door. She pulled on her nightshirt, slid under the covers and arranged her mosquito net over her mattress, then lay down to wait. Five minutes later he was back, his body beaded with moisture from the *mandi*, the sarong clinging to his damp body and leaving little to the imagination.

She dragged her eyes away and hauled in a breath, and turned firmly on her side away from him. 'I think you're being ridiculous. We've got a security guard—'

'Who's asleep again. I just checked. He's about as much use as a eunuch in a brothel.'

'That's disgusting.'

'Oh, Gabby, give over. We need some rest. Your virtue's safe. Just go to sleep.'

She couldn't, though, not for ages. She lay and listened to every creak, every scream and wail from the jungle just yards away, and then there were the soft snores that drifted out from under Jed's makeshift mosquito net.

Dawn seemed to take ages to break, and when it did she fell into a deep and dreamless sleep. Jed woke her at nine with a cup of tea and the news that he and Jon were going up to the compound to look around, and he was then going back to town to continue his sleuthing.

'More people who owe you favours?' she asked without any real rancour, and he grinned.

'Comes in handy at times. I'll see you later.'

The day dragged without him around. She spent most of it with Penny, trying to amuse the children and distract them and Penny from their worries. Despite her protests of the previous day, Penny was packing to leave the island, taking just a few things and going to Jakarta with the children for a while until things settled down. She persuaded Gabby to pack and come with her and, as she could see little point in staying without Penny, she agreed.

They were to leave late next morning on the little local plane. Jon was relieved that they had both seen sense, and Jed, too, nodded his agreement when he came back at ten that night. They talked with Bill, the developer, for some time, and then Jed rose to his feet and stretched.

'Bedtime,' he said to the assembled company. 'Tomorrow could be quite eventful.'

Gabby was happy to agree. The sleepless night before had taken its toll, and she slept like a log, comforted this time by Jed's presence.

He'd said nothing about what he'd discovered the previous day, but he'd had a thoughtful look on his face, and she wasn't surprised when she woke at dawn and found he was gone. She slid her feet over the edge of the bed, ducked under the mosquito net and padded softly out into the sitting-room area in the centre of the bungalow. She could hear him moving around in his bedroom, and she looked through the open door to see him packing medicines into a flight bag.

'What are you doing?' she asked.

His head whipped round and he searched her eyes, as if he wasn't sure how much to tell her.

Eventually he spoke, measuring every word. 'Derek needs insulin. The others need anti-malarials, probably antibiotics and anti-inflammatories, and there could be all sorts of other emergencies—dysentery, fungal infections, burns and wounds that won't heal—the jungle's a nasty place.'

'And how do you intend to get this little Red Cross parcel to them?' Gabby asked, plopping down on the edge of a chest and waiting.

He hesitated again, and she felt a sinking feeling inside. 'You're going to try and go to them, aren't you?' she said, following her unerring nurse's instinct.

'There's a scout gone up there—he may be able to get a message to them.'

'And pigs fly. You're going to walk up there, aren't you, if you can get an idea of where it is?'

He sighed and sat back on his heels. 'Yes. I think I stand a better chance of negotiating than your cousin or Bill and, anyway, I'm a bachelor. It's reasonable I should be the one to go.'

'And how will you know the way?'

He shifted, and she fixed him with a steely glare. 'How, Jed?'

'Jamal knows a man from there—he's an outcast, but he knows the way. He'll be able to show me how to get there. We'll set off later this morning.'

'So why didn't you tell Jon last night?'

He laughed softly. 'Because he would have had a fit, and so would Penny. I went up with Bill yesterday to fly over the site and see what we could see but, as I suspected, it was nothing. Before they get up I want to go and look at the site from the ground—the compound, the area where they've been drilling and blasting for the feasibility study—all of it. See if I can work out what the problem is.'

'Can I come?'

He quirked a brow. 'Can't keep away from me?'

She blushed. 'Not at all. I just thought two pairs of eyes might be better than one, and our plane doesn't go for ages.'

'Do you know what to look for?'

'Do you?'

He shrugged in submission and grinned. 'No, not really. It might just be a holy place—there might be nothing *to* see. I just want to look, that's all—and, yes, you can come if you're ready now.'

She glanced down at her nightshirt. 'Give me ten seconds.'

She was back in about ninety, just as he put the last of his pills and potions into the flight bag and zipped it up. 'I'll take this with me—there are one or two things up at the compound I need to pick up as well.'

The Jeep, bursting into life, woke the security guard with a start, and he grinned and waved and rubbed his eyes.

'What a waste of a good skin,' Jed muttered, and gunned the engine.

Gabby said nothing. She was too busy hanging on like

grim death because Jed clearly didn't intend to waste any time on this trip. They hurtled up to the compound, disturbing another security guard who slept peacefully in the shade of a veranda, and then, after collecting a few more drugs and supplies from the infirmary and making a cursory check around the immediate area, they set off again for the proposed site of the power station.

It wasn't far, a third of a mile at the most, but the road was every bit as bad as the other one, and as they grew nearer so it became worse, more winding and twisting as they negotiated rocky outcrops and the huge trunks of fallen trees.

Finally Jed pulled the Jeep up in a little clearing and turned off the ignition. The silence was deafening. Gradually, sounds began to return—birds screeching, monkeys whooping and yelling, the chirring of the cicadas, and underlying it all the dull roar of water. The sounds all seemed distant, though, as if there was an uneasy silence over the area.

'Come on,' he said briskly, and slid out from behind the wheel. She followed him, almost running to keep up with his long stride, and then finally they emerged on the edge of a rocky cliff.

Below them, falling almost vertically for fifty feet or more, the river crashed downwards towards Telok Panjang and the sea, a foaming torrent of water that threw up a veil of mist. Gabby could quite see how harnessing its power would provide electricity for the town and the new resort.

'The plan is to divert some of the water over here, and build a turbine house to take the generators,' Jed yelled over the roar of the waterfall. 'That will mean damming it and putting weirs in the side of the lake— it might be that there's something here that's sacred. Let's take a look.'

They retreated from the edge of the cliff, to Gabby's relief, and studied the area Jed indicated. A little lake lay sparkling in the sunlight, a natural weir-pool and the perfect pick-up point for the water they would need to power the turbines.

It was beautiful, peaceful and cool and restful, and there didn't seem to be anything—any artefacts or man-made structures—that could be shrines or tombs or any such thing that might be of significance. The only strange thing was the wonderful peace she felt steal over her as she stood there in the dim light of the jungle.

Gabby tipped her head and looked up through the soaring trunks of the jungle giants that fringed the edges of the lake. They were amazing, great gnarled trees with massive boles and leaves so far removed from the roots she wondered how they could possibly pump the water such a long way.

Some of them had a strange chequered effect on the bark—an almost square pattern of astonishing symmetry that clothed the lower part of the trunks.

She nudged Jed. 'Look at those trees—the bark's really weird.'

He looked, and his eyes narrowed for a second. 'My God—I think that might be the answer.'

'What might?'

He looked at her, his eyes strangely bright in the artificial twilight. 'Grave trees,' he said.

'What?'

'They have them in Tanatoraja, in Sulawesi. They're animists, too, and it's possible the two tribes could be related. One might be an offshoot of the other. Whatever. They believe that if infants die without touching the earth their souls go directly to heaven, and so for the first few months of their lives they're carried everywhere and never put down. If a baby dies they cut a hole in the bark of a grave tree, chisel out a cavity and put the baby's body inside, then replace the bark and put a little door over the hole. That way the baby never has to touch the ground.'

Gabby swallowed. 'So those trees contain dead babies?'

He peered closely at them. 'Could be.'

She laid a hand over her chest, conscious of a great feeling of sadness. A cold chill ran over her. 'Oh, Jed. No wonder they want to protect them.'

'They're right in the line of the turbine house and the weirs. They'd have to be felled without a doubt if the plant was to be sited here.'

'But it can't!' Gabby protested. 'They can't be allowed to cut them down!'

'They could be hundreds of years old. Those marks aren't new by any stretch of the imagination, Gabby. It might be a red herring.'

She knew it wasn't, though, just as she knew that the strange feeling of peace came from the souls of those children.

Tears welled in her eyes. 'Jed, they can't cut them down, no matter how old they are. They must be left in peace.'

He turned to her, saw her tears and cupped her face gently in his big hands, smoothing the tears away with his thumbs. 'I think I'll let you negotiate with Bill. He's a sucker for pretty women.'

She smacked his hands away and turned, wrapping her arms around her chest. 'I mean it. They can't be allowed to desecrate this area, Jed. Can't you feel it?'

His hands closed over her shoulders. 'Oh, yes, I can feel it. I agree with you. I'm just wondering how Bill will feel about all the money he's spent on this project so far, and how much it would cost to relocate it.'

'Tough,' Gabby said uncompromisingly.

Jed squeezed her shoulders and she heard a soft laugh. 'I think we'll definitely let you tell him.'

Her shoulders drooped, and he eased her back against his chest and rubbed the tense muscles of her neck with his thumbs. 'We'll talk to him. With the lives of the others on line I'm sure he'll see reason—if we're right and that is the problem.'

She looked up at the trees again, and sighed. 'Why didn't anybody notice before?'

'Because nobody was looking. The area's uninhabited now—Jamal told me the hill tribe moved north years ago when the Dutch arrived. What seemed like a natural clearing where we parked the Jeep is probably the site of the old village. This graveyard is all of a hundred years old, if not more.'

'That doesn't stop it being sacred.'

'No, but nevertheless I don't suppose anyone was looking for grave trees when they did the feasibility studies. Like I said, they're exclusively Torajan, or I thought they were. Obviously these people have never been studied.'

'Perhaps because of their powerful magic?'

'Maybe.'

'Or perhaps just because they're very fierce.'

His hands fell to his sides. 'Perhaps. Come on, let's get back and tell Jon.'

They turned, and then stopped dead. Five men stood around the Jeep, naked except for bark loincloths and tattoos. Their skins were smeared with what looked like ash, and they held long things in their hands, not spears but something else. Blowpipes?

'Hell,' Jed said quietly.

'I'll go for that,' Gabby mumbled from beside him.

One of the men stepped forwards. '*Docktor?*'

Jed nodded and pointed to his chest. '*Docktor*,' he repeated.

The man jabbed his blowpipe upriver, at a barely discernible path in the jungle. '*Jalan-jalan*,' he growled.

'I don't think he's negotiating,' Gabby said softly.

'No. I'll take the medicine and go with them, you get in the Jeep and go like hell for the town. Tell them what we've found out, and start the negotiations rolling. OK? And get them to follow us.'

She nodded, and he winked. 'Attagirl.'

He stepped forward, picked up the bag from the Jeep and turned to the waiting men. As he moved, Gabby got into the Jeep and reached for the ignition, but there was a yell and one of them pulled her out. There was an urgent exchange, and she felt the press of cold steel at her back.

'I think they want me to come too,' she said as steadily as she could manage. Her heart was pounding, her mouth was dry and she thought her legs were about to give way, but she was damned if any of them would know that.

She lifted her chin a notch and noted the approval in Jed's eyes. A lot of good that would do her.

'No problem. I'll try and talk to them.'

He spoke in Bahasa, then in the native dialect of Pulau Panjang, but he was met with a blank wall of silence. Incomprehension, or just a stubborn refusal to listen?

The ringleader jabbed his blowpipe at Gabby. '*Jalan-jalan*,' he repeated, sounding angry now, and the man holding her thrust her forward so that she staggered against Jed.

They were looking at the flight bag, and Jed unzipped it. '*Obat*,' he told them. Medicine. They nodded, and they turned towards the jungle. Three of them went first, melting into the jungle along an almost invisible path. Jed turned to her. 'Stay close,' he ordered.

The others fell in behind, and within seconds the undergrowth closed in behind them and the last trace of civilisation vanished...

CHAPTER FIVE

IT TOOK Gabby about two seconds to work out that if they went any further into the jungle she wouldn't be able to find her way back to the Jeep.

It took about another two seconds to tell herself it was a crazy idea, but so what? So she was crazy. So they had blowpipes. One quick poison dart was probably preferable to walking all day in the jungle in nothing but a pair of thin trousers, trainers and a long-sleeved shirt.

She was too hot, and she'd already discovered that the trousers gave little protection against the whipping stems of some of the more vicious jungle plants she'd already encountered—and they'd hardly started their journey, she was sure of that! And, anyway, she might be the last chance the hostages had. She had to get back to Jon and explain about the grave trees and do something positive before the situation escalated out of control.

She scuffed her shoe heel down, loosened it, then casually walked out of it and stopped dead. As she bent over to refasten it Jed and three of their captors had moved ahead, and there were only the two men following her.

They looked reasonably harmless, she thought, if one ignored the blowpipes and nose-bones. She smiled and made a great production of putting her shoe on again, then, as the others disappeared from view ahead of them, she turned and threw herself against one, catching him by surprise and knocking him over. Using her old netball skills, she ducked past the other and ran back down the path towards the Jeep.

At least, she'd meant to, but in her haste the jungle blurred into a mat of foliage and the path vanished. She pushed the stems aside, hurling herself forwards against the vegetation to cleave a path through it, and ran straight into a mass of thorny stems.

The vicious spikes ripped her clothes and skin, and with a scream of frustration and pain she fought to free herself.

Hands stopped her, trapping her arms and pulling her backwards out of the savage clutches of the monster plant and back against a hard, muscled chest. The arms were like steel bands, and once she was free of the plant they half dragged, half carried her back towards the others.

'Let me go!' she protested, but the arms didn't move and she was propelled relentlessly back through the undergrowth, kicking and screaming.

Not that it did any good. Her captor's arms simply tightened and, apart from a grunt of pain when her heel connected with his shin, she slowed him down so little she might as well have been a gnat.

She could hear yelling in the distance, and as they neared the rest of the group she was released and thrust forward so that she fell at the feet of the ringleader.

'That was a bit bloody stupid,' Jed said angrily, and, ignoring the men, he pulled her roughly to her feet, hauled her up against him and hit her hard across the face.

She screamed, blood trickling down her lip, and raised her fists to pound on his chest. He caught them with one large hand, trapped them and then glared at her—but not angrily. 'Don't say a word,' he growled. 'Just play along. You're my wife, you do as I tell you, I'm responsible for you. It's the only way you'll be safe.'

'The Indonesian didn't hit me,' she grated back at him.

'No, he's just ready to rape you, and if you get away from the others again he probably will. He's looking at you as if he'd like to eat you. Now cast your eyes down, look ashamed and I'll try and explain that you're a difficult wife but I'm taming you gradually.'

He pulled her round to his side none too gently, looked at the boss-man and gave a man-to-man shrug, then he grasped a vine and indicated to one of the men that he would like it chopped. With a quick twisting motion he wound it around her right wrist and shackled her to his left.

'What the hell are you doing?' she muttered furiously.

'Ensuring your safety and proving that you're my chattel. Now shut up!' He held up their wrists, rolled his eyes expressively and winked.

To her relief and fury, they laughed and the party set off again. There was no further chance of escape, of course, but it seemed there was none anyway so she probably hadn't lost anything except her dignity and several inches of skin.

Bitter disappointment settled like a lead weight in her chest, and gradually as the sweat trickled down her body into the cuts and scratches the pain became almost unbearable. Her mouth hurt where he'd hit her, the vine was chafing on her wrist and she was sick of trailing just behind Jed with one arm outstretched to accommodate her shackle. It wasn't necessary anyway, she thought crossly, but at least, being so close behind him, his big body took most of the sting from the undergrowth.

Then she stumbled over a root and fell, only Jed's arm tied to hers preventing her from falling right down.

A little sob broke from her lips, and he turned and helped her up again, then tipped her chin and winked at her.

'Keep going,' he murmured comfortingly. 'You're doing well.'

'Liar,' she grumbled.

'I'm sorry about your face. I had to make it look real.'

'That real?' she said bitterly.

His thumb brushed the bruise on her swollen lip. 'I'll make it up to you. Just hang on in there, it can't last for ever—the island's not that big.'

But it was, of course. She'd seen it from the air, and she knew just how big it was. Anyway, distances couldn't be measured in normal ways because progress was so slow.

She tried a smile, and he dropped a hard, quick kiss on her lips and turned away again. As he did she caught the eyes of the man who'd chased her, and realised with a chill that Jed had been right. His eyes were glittering with a strange fever, and she just knew that given the slightest chance he'd try and get her alone.

Which was a problem because just then she wanted to be alone, just for a moment or two. She tugged at Jed.

'I need the loo,' she hissed.

'Fine. Can you hang on? They have to stop soon.'

'I hope you're right.'

They trudged on, however. The heat was relentless, steamy and intolerable. Her mouth was dry, and she thought she'd have given her eye teeth for a long glass of ice-cold beer.

She began to fantasise about it, to such an extent that when their captors called a halt she didn't even notice and cannoned into Jed's hot, sweaty back.

It was probably no hotter and sweatier than her front

so she leant against it, exhausted, and waited for some instructions.

As she listened she heard the sound of rushing water, and realised they were still near the river. The cold, wet, clean, thirst-quenching river—

'I think he's saying we can drink and bathe, and I think they've got some food,' Jed said softly over his shoulder.

She straightened and looked around, and found they were in a little clearing beside the river. The air was cooler, and the water looked wonderful. Just then the men disappeared one at a time and came back, adjusting their loinclothes.

'Jed, I need to go!' she muttered. 'Take this thing off—'

'No. We'll go together.'

Jed waved his arms about in some ghastly sign language, and the ringleader nodded. Unfortunately he also accompanied them out of the clearing, standing over them with his arms folded.

'Jed, I can't—'

'I think you're going to have to. I'll stand between you and him.'

'What makes you think you're any better than he is? Jed, I want a private pee! Is that so much to ask?'

He grinned. 'If it's any consolation so do I, and I'm not going to get one. I'll turn round and face him, and you can turn your back to me—'

'Can't you just untie me?' she pleaded for the nth time, but he was emphatic about it.

She was too hot and tired to flounce so she turned round and then discovered the impossibility of undoing her clothes with her left hand and squatting down over prickly undergrowth full of unmentionable creepy-crawlies—

With a yelp she catapulted to her feet, forgetting the shackle and almost dragging Jed over on top of her.

'What the hell?' He turned towards her to steady her, and then looked down. 'You've forgotten something.'

She yanked up her knickers and trousers and to her embarrassment had to enlist Jed's help in refastening them.

'Want to tell me what that was all about?' he asked calmly when she was reassembled.

'I felt something tickling me,' she muttered, furiously embarrassed.

'Is that all?' he asked with a chuckle. 'I thought at the very least you'd been bitten on the bottom by a cobra.'

Her eyes widened. 'A what?'

'Forget it. I needed cheering up.'

'At my expense?'

There was a wicked twinkle in his eye and if she hadn't been so damn tired she would have hit him. As it was she leant her head on his chest for a second, then straightened again, tilted her chin and nodded.

'Any chance of a wash?' she said wistfully.

Again Jed went through the pantomime, and they were led through the trees to the river. It tumbled over rocks, looking clear and cool and absolutely the best thing in the world to Gabby, and she almost fell into it in her haste.

'Steady,' Jed murmured, and then he was beside her on the rocks, sloshing water over his head and face with one hand while the other went up and down to hers, shackled to her arm.

One particular scratch was stinging furiously, and she turned back her cuff to look at it.

'When did you do that?'

'When I tried to play the hero,' she said drily. 'There was a great spiky vine thing—'

'Rattan. It's wicked. Let me look.'

He rolled up her sleeves, tutting and mumbling, and washed all the scratches thoroughly—too thoroughly in some cases. Then he rolled up her trouser legs and did the same thing with those, and by the time he'd finished and smeared antiseptic over them from his box of tricks the hill men were looking bored and irritated.

They were each handed a little bunch of bright yellow fig-shaped fruits, and then nudged on the way.

'Can't we sit and rest?' Gabby pleaded, but apparently they couldn't.

She fell in behind Jed, examining the fruits with suspicion. 'What do you suppose they are?'

'Figs. They'll probably give you the runs, but they taste good.'

The runs? While she was shackled to him and in front of an audience? Not in this lifetime!

She lobbed them into the forest and trudged on, ignoring the rumbling of her stomach. She'd rather starve than go through that.

Four hours later she was regretting her impulse. They'd had another quick pitstop, but there was nothing else to eat and she thought if she didn't wrap herself around something substantial soon she was going to fade right away.

Melt, in fact. She remembered the old saying, 'Ladies glow, men perspire, pigs sweat.' Clearly she was a pig.

A tired pig. She put one foot in front of the other without any real awareness of where she was going, except that she was following Jed. She couldn't see for the sweat and dirt that was running down her face, although that was probably marginally preferable to the rain that had fallen. The air was still soaked, a fine misting drizzle falling from the canopy, and every third or fourth step some kind-hearted leaf generously poured a couple of pints of water down the back of her neck as she went underneath, but at least the unrelenting downpour had stopped.

The path was slippery now, and there was something on her wrist which she had an idea was a leech.

'They're medicinal,' she told herself, and ignored it. Some while later it had dropped off, and there was a little red spot where it had been, with a thin trail of blood leaking from it.

'I'm going to bleed to death and Jed won't know until he looks round and finds my corpse, dangling behind his wrist,' she mumbled.

He stopped dead and she crashed into his back. 'What?'

'Nothing. I'm bleeding to death.'

He turned abruptly. 'What? Where?'

She showed him her wrist, and he gave a huff of laughter that sounded suspiciously relieved and ruffled her hair. 'Chin up. You're doing fine. Look, we must be nearly at the village, the path's much clearer now.'

She looked and, lo and behold, she could actually see where they were heading for the first time since they'd set off on their tortuous journey.

Not that she'd been exactly looking hard.

'Yippee,' she said expressionlessly, and he gave her a quick hug and turned back, setting off again. Their captors, who had stood patiently waiting during this exchange, picked up the pace and within minutes they were surrounded by a group of chattering children, darting back and forth and giggling.

'This must be it,' Jed murmured, and moments later they were in a clearing in the forest. A few large huts clustered around the fringes under the shade of the canopy, simple huts roofed with leaves of some sort, capable of sleeping several families.

The families themselves were standing round, studying them, their bodies all smeared with ash like their captors', and then into the throng came a white woman Gabby had never met.

'Jed—oh, thank God!' she wept, and threw herself at him.

He hugged her, a little awkwardly because of the shackle that still tied him to Gabby, and then eased her away. 'How are you, Sue?'

'Sick as a pig but that's just because of the baby. Derek's awful—I don't suppose by a miracle you've got any insulin?'

He nodded, and Sue's eyes closed with relief. 'Thank God—he's almost in a coma, Jed. Come on...'

She started to drag him forward, and together they were herded into one of the huts. They had to climb a ladder to reach the entrance. Once inside it was gloomy and Gabby had to blink and screw up her eyes to see.

What she saw did nothing for her. Derek was pale and sweating, his eyes sunken in his grey and slightly stubbled face, and his breath was an instant give-away.

'Pear drops—his blood sugar must be sky high,' Gabby mumbled, and Jed nodded. Kneeling down beside the sick man, Jed untied the vine from his wrist to free Gabby, told her to stay close and quickly examined him.

'Has he been vomiting?'

'Yes.'

'Drowsy?'

'Yes—and slurred speech. He sounds drunk—well, he did. He hasn't spoken for an hour or so, but I don't think he's in a coma. I can rouse him still, just about,' Sue told them.

Jed passed Gabby the bag of goodies and asked her

to pull up a very high dose of insulin, about twice or three times the normal amount. This was to deal with the high level of blood sugar that was causing Derek's symptoms and would push him before long, if Gabby wasn't mistaken, into a coma.

She'd seen diabetic comas, both hypo- and hyperglycaemic, and knew exactly what to do. It was a good job she did because she was definitely on autopilot.

She drew up the insulin and looked at what Jed was doing. Her eyes widened when she saw the dark green-blue of the testing stick on which he had put a drop of Derek's blood.

'That's dark.'

'Almost black. It's well off the scale, which goes up to 44. Normal should be about 8. That's what I'm aiming for in the next twenty-four hours. Got that insulin ready?'

She handed him the syringe and watched as he injected it. 'There—he should be feeling better in an hour or so, and within twenty-four hours he should be fine.'

He looked up. 'What about the rest of you?'

The three Indonesian engineers were sitting around on the other side of Derek, watching Jed anxiously. At his question one proffered a foot with a nasty cut on the ankle, but that was the only problem. Jed cleaned it and squirted it with antibiotic spray, gave him an injection of antibiotics and dished out anti-malarials to everyone. Then finally, when everyone had been seen to, he turned to Sue.

'We need to wash and have some food—how strictly are you guarded?'

She gave a hollow laugh. 'Guarded? Where would we go?' She scrambled to her feet. 'Come with me, I'll show you where you can wash—have you got any clean clothes?'

He shook his head. 'No. Nothing except the drugs, by a miracle. I was just getting them ready in case I got a chance to get them up to you somehow, and we'd just collected the last few things from the compound. They took us from the power-station site—and I've got something to tell you about that, as well, after we've washed. I don't suppose you could rustle up some food?'

'Sure. It might be a little strange but none of us have been sick yet. They seem to be taking good care of us. They've almost been hospitable, crazy though it seems. I don't think they want to harm us.'

'No. I don't think they do—I think that's why they came for me. They must have been waiting at the compound and followed us on foot.'

'They knew Derek was sick right from the start. He grabbed what insulin he could, but of course there wasn't enough up at the compound and it ran out yesterday morning. They seemed to understand he was ill, and we saw the men who brought you leaving the village by the path we'd come on. They might have had time to get down there before dark.'

Jed nodded. 'Makes sense. Without us they would have made better time, and downhill as well would have been easier.'

Gabby wasn't sure about that. She almost fell down the ladder she was so tired, but the sight of a clear pool in the rocks at the foot of a long sloping waterfall was enough to wake her up. 'Let me in,' she mumbled, and, pulling off her shoes, she walked straight into the water without stopping.

It was freezing on her hot skin, but the pain of her scratches and bites faded instantly and she lay back in the water with a sigh of relief and shut her eyes.

'Wow,' Jed murmured from beside her, and disappeared under the water for endless seconds. He came up just when she was starting to panic, shooting up through the surface and shaking his head like a dog, sending water droplets flying.

Then he grinned, and he looked as fresh as a daisy.

She wanted to kill him.

She also wanted another bathroom stop, but she thought she might wait and ask Sue about that. She sluiced her hair again, squeezed the water out of it and then wondered what to do about her dripping clothes.

'Take them off and wring them out, then put them back on. They'll soon dry and they'll keep you cool.'

She gave him a sideways glance and saw he was following his own advice, standing on the rocks at the edge of the pool in a pair of skimpy briefs, looking more delicious than he had any right to look after the day they'd just gone through.

She pulled herself out of the water, peeled off the sodden clothes and squeezed them out and then, after her skin had stopped streaming, she went to put them on again.

'Hang on.'

Jed's hands touched her gently, turning her this way and that in the soft green light, and he shook his head. 'You're a mess—why didn't you say how bad the scratches were?'

She shrugged, standing there in her soggy undies, all but naked. 'What would you have done—admitted me to hospital? It wouldn't have made any difference.'

He looked at her and through her bleary haze she thought she saw respect in his eyes. 'Come on,' he said gently, and helped her into her clothes. He had scratches and bites too, she noticed as she returned the favour. He hadn't said anything either. She promised herself she'd put some cream on them once they were back at the hut.

Sue was waiting for them. She showed them what

passed for a bathroom, then on their return greeted them with some food—vegetables baked in leaves, boiled rice and some sauce, which Gabby avoided because it smelt so strongly of chilli she thought it would finish her off.

The meal was strange but palatable, and as they ate it darkness fell. The temperature fell with it, dropping sharply up here in the hills as it didn't nearer the coast. She remembered climbing Ben Nevis once and being astonished at the temperature difference. Somehow in the tropics she just hadn't expected it.

Someone lit a candle, a makeshift affair that smelt vile but probably kept the mosquitoes out. By its meagre light Jed told the others about the grave trees they had found. The Indonesians particularly were very excited at this.

'I think it must be the reason they want us to stop,' Luther said. 'They have been chanting and the priest has been wearing ceremonial robes and dancing and they sacrificed a pig today. I think they are using their strongest magic.'

'All we need to do is tell the others,' Sue said. 'Got any bright ideas?'

Jed grinned and, like a conjurer pulling a rabbit out of a hat, he produced a thing like a mobile phone from the bottom of the flight bag.

'The Magellan GCS! Jed, you're wonderful!' Sue cried.

'What?' Gabby asked, confused. 'Surely a mobile phone won't work.'

'No, it won't—but this will. It's a global communications system, and I can send an e-mail to anywhere in the world, telling them where we are and what's going on. All I have to do is remember the e-mail number—and that's the problem. I can't. The only one I can remember is my own, and I don't know if anyone will check my e-mail at work, or how often. My secretary might, but perhaps not for a day or two. Still, it's the best chance we've got.'

He keyed in a few brief words about the grave trees, their reunion with the other hostages and their state of health, and sent the message winging on its way, before shutting the machine down. 'I must keep the batteries going as long as possible—we have no idea how long we'll be here,' he told them all. 'If I remember a more relevant number I'll try sending our whereabouts to that.'

'Our whereabouts?' Gabby said with a laugh. 'A jungle hut in the middle of God knows where? How precise.'

'It is. It's a satellite GPS—a global positioning system. It tells them where we are to within fifteen metres.'

Gabby's jaw dropped. 'It's that precise, and you've just done it? Just like that?'

He nodded.

'So they might come and rescue us?'

He looked thoughtful.

'Well? Will they?' she pressed.

'Yes—when the message is picked up. And that's the problem. I don't know when the message will be picked up, or even if it will. I'm sorry.'

'Doesn't it have a memory for addresses?' Sue asked.

'Yes—but I haven't got round to programming them in yet. I've only had it a few days.'

Sue's face fell. 'It isn't Derek's?'

Jed shook his head, and she dropped her face into her hands for a moment. When she straightened she looked calm but tired. 'I suppose we'll just have to wait, then,' she said pragmatically. 'It can't take for ever. How much insulin did you bring?'

'Enough for two weeks.'

Sue perked up immediately. 'Well, it won't be that long, will it?' she said more brightly, and then turned to Derek. 'How are you?' she asked him.

'Horrible—I need Jed.'

'Jed's here—he's brought his Magellan. We're going to be all right, Derek. They'll find us soon. It's OK, love, we're going to be all right.'

Gabby, hearing the optimism in the other woman's voice, felt a cold shiver of fear run over her. Perhaps it was her still-damp clothes, or perhaps the fact that two weeks wasn't really all that long in the great scheme of things. If the e-mail didn't get picked up—

'OK?'

Jed's voice was soft and right beside her, and she looked up at him and tried to smile.

'I'll be better once I've got some cream on these scratches and I can go to sleep,' she told him.

'Easily done. I gather we're all sleeping here together in this hut. The men are together in one part, then Sue and Derek, and we get the last bit. We'll stick to the myth that we're married—you'll be safer that way.'

'Definitely,' Sue assured them. 'They might not want to do us any harm, but there are plenty of healthy young men here who would be fascinated to sleep with a white woman. I think telling them you're married is an excellent idea.'

Gabby yawned and Jed unfolded himself and stood up, then pulled her to her feet. 'We'll go and settle down now. See you in the morning. Call me if you're worried about Derek—I've given him another shot of insulin and his blood sugar level's falling steadily. I think he'll be all right soon.'

They padded along the little corridor to the room at the end, a small area screened off by a beaten bark curtain over the doorway, and in the middle of the floor was a heap of bedding—rush mats, sarongs and a couple of woven rugs.

They sorted out the beds and Gabby took off her outer clothes, pulled on the sarong she'd been left and fastened it. Then Jed, as much by touch as by sight, spread cream over her lacerated arms and legs, and around her wrist where the vine had cut in during the day.

'You're a mess,' he said huskily, and she remembered the sun cream. It seemed weeks ago—months. In fact, it had been only forty-eight hours earlier. She was exhausted, she had aches where she hadn't known she had muscles, and yet at his touch her body seemed to find another life.

She felt the pain ebbing, the aches soothing, and a mellow warmth seeped through her. She lay bonelessly, letting him move her arms and legs around, rolling onto her front when he prodded her, and all she could think about was the feel of his hand on her skin.

All too soon he stopped, and she rolled over and looked up at him in the darkness. A candle was burning in the little passage outside, and in its dim light she could make out his shadowed features. She reached up a hand and cupped his cheek.

'Thanks,' she murmured languorously.

He capped the tube and turned away. 'You're welcome.'

'How about you?'

He made a choked sound and looked back at her over his shoulder. 'How about me?'

'Want me to do your scratches?'

He looked at her for endless moments, before turning away. 'I'll do them. You rest.'

She lay and watched him, then took the tube and did his shoulders and back, anyway, where the occasional particularly determined vine had coiled round him. His skin was hot, like damp silk, and she had to struggle to resist the urge to lay her lips against it—

'That'll do,' he muttered, and his voice sounded slightly strangled.

She lay back and watched as he got ready for bed, then lay down beside her. The noises of the jungle seemed incredibly loud and close, and they could hear the shufflings and soft snores of the others on the other side of the wall.

He turned his head towards her. 'You did well today, Gabby,' he said quietly. 'Well done.'

'What about you? You must have been exhausted when we arrived, but you dealt with Derek straight away.'

He laughed softly. 'I didn't think Derek had time to wait while we freshened up—and, anyway, you helped.'

'Only a bit. I don't think I could have walked any further, though,' she told him.

'No, nor me. Good job we didn't have to.' His hand reached out and squeezed her shoulder. ''Night,' he said softly.

'Goodnight.' She turned on her side to face him, but she didn't sleep. Tired as she was, too much had happened for her to relax. She lay for ages, then she thought she heard him sigh.

'Jed?' she whispered.

'Mmm?'

'I can't sleep.'

'I can't sleep either,' he murmured. 'Too much to think about.'

The candle had gone out, and in the darkness the noises all seemed louder. Knowing the others were close by was strangely comforting, but she still felt very alone. She wriggled a little closer to Jed. It was chilly now, and she wished she'd got something a little thicker than the mat and a sarong and little woven rug to cover her.

'Penny will be worried sick,' she said.

'If she knows. She might have thought you'd changed your mind, and gone without you. Jon and Bill will be worrying, though, and I expect the chief of police will put another dozy security guard on the case, for all the good it'll do.'

Gabby thought back to their capture and the appearance of the men in the clearing by the Jeep. 'I wonder how they knew who you were and where to find you?'

'They have their contacts, I expect—Jamal's exile friend for one. Anyway, it's a good job they did. Without medical help for Derek, he would have been dead in twenty-four hours. I expect they realised how sick he was and couldn't afford to risk him dying. Anyway, as Sue said, they don't seem to mean us any harm.'

Gabby gave a hollow laugh. 'I wish I had your confidence. My legs and arms certainly feel harmed, and my feet are killing me.'

He laughed gently at her, then reached out a hand. 'Are you warm enough?'

'Not really.'

'Nor am I. Come over here and warm up.'

She hesitated for a nanosecond—certainly not long enough for decency—and then shuffled across the mats to his side. He pulled her light covering across them both, tucked her bottom into his lap and draped an arm round her waist. 'Better?' he murmured.

'Mmm.' She snuggled closer, comforted by the solid warmth of his body at her back, and fell instantly asleep.

CHAPTER SIX

GABBY woke to find her head cradled on Jed's shoulder, her hair spread across his chest and cramp in her foot.

'Ow,' she moaned, and he pitched her off him and sat bolt upright.

'Wha—?'

She flapped a hand at him to shush him. 'Nothing exciting,' she whispered. 'I've got cramp.' She folded over and grabbed the offending foot, and Jed took it from her and stretched the toes up towards her knee, straightening her leg and pulling the muscles tight in her arch. Then he dug his thumb into the offending muscle and she wailed softly.

Pig that he was, he laughed at her, a kindly laugh but a laugh for all that. She decided he needed punishing so she put her foot in the middle of his chest and pushed.

Unfortunately he still had hold of her foot so he didn't fall. Instead a dangerous glint appeared in his eyes and he dodged her foot and sprawled across her, pinning her to the floor, his stubbled face hovering just inches from hers.

'Want to play games, do you?' he asked softly, and there was a curious rasp to his voice that did crazy things to her nerves.

She couldn't move, couldn't speak, couldn't do anything. She was trapped, pinned down as much by the look in his eyes as by his arms. Against her leg she felt his body stir, coming to life in response to her closeness, and with a tiny moan she closed her eyes and accepted his kiss. His beard scraped her face softly, sensitising her skin further, making her forget common sense.

Her sarong had ridden up around her hips and he shifted, one hard-muscled thigh nudging between her legs and settling against the ache that was growing with every touch of his lips on hers. She was conscious of the coarse, wiry hair against the tender skin of her thighs, the contrast of his hard, masculine frame aligned with her softer, more yielding body.

He shifted so he could gain access to her breasts, tugging the sarong down and closing one large, hard hand over her softness. She had never felt so much a woman, or been touched by so much a man. She arched against him, against that thigh that chafed with such devastating accuracy against her, and as she did so the cramp that had woken her returned with interest.

She wrenched her mouth from his with a yelp and reached for her foot, and he rolled away and took it from her, stretching and kneading it again in a strained silence broken only by their ragged breathing.

Finally, when the knot had dissolved and her foot was relaxed again, he set it down with great care and looked at her.

His eyes were smouldering, and she was suddenly aware of the sarong rucked up around her waist, the top unfastened to expose the soft swell of her breasts...

She covered herself hastily and sat up, pushing the hair out of her eyes, and saw him withdraw into himself.

'Saved by the bell, eh?' he murmured softly.

He stood up and turned away from her, but not before she'd seen that he was still aroused. His briefs hid nothing, and the ache returned, slamming into her so hard that she had to bite back the moan that rose in her throat.

He pulled on his clothes, slid his feet into his shoes

and went out, leaving her sitting there in the midst of their bedding, frustration her only companion.

She could hear the others moving about, and next door through the thin bamboo wall she could hear Jed murmuring to Derek and Sue.

Had they heard everything? Oh, Lord. She buried her face in her hands and sighed. Why had she tried to push him over? When would she learn not to bait the tiger?

She scrambled to her feet, pulled on her clothes and dragged her fingers through her hair. Then, on the principle of getting unpleasant things over and out of the way, she went along the hut to the end where Sue and Derek were sitting, staring out of the doorway.

'How's the patient?' she asked brightly, avoiding Jed's eyes.

'Which one?' Sue said weakly. 'Derek's better but any second now I'm going to throw up.'

'No, you're not,' Jed said reassuringly. 'Come on, have some fruit. That'll stay down.'

Gabby saw they had fruit and cold rice and bamboo tubes filled with coconut milk set out on the floor in front of them. As they settled down to eat, Sue eyed the food with horror and then covered her mouth.

She leapt to her feet and ran, threw herself down the ladder and fell to her knees in the dirt, retching helplessly.

'Ginger,' Jed said, standing with Gabby in the doorway of the hut and regarding the poor woman dispassionately, a banana skin dangling from his fingers.

'Ginger?' Gabby repeated.

'Mmm. Good anti-emetic. It's used a lot now for travel sickness. I wonder if we can get any—would you like to ask the women? They might know.'

She stared at his retreating back. Ask the women. Just like that. No language barrier, of course!

She went down the ladder to Sue, put a comforting arm round her shoulders and helped her back to her bed, then went out into the village again. A pregnant woman was sitting with her back propped against the stilts of her house, pounding something in a coconut shell.

She was beautiful, her black hair long and lustrous, her flawless skin a deep golden brown. She was wearing only a loosely woven skirt, slung around her hips under the prominent swelling of her baby, and Gabby approached her with a cautious smile.

The woman put down her makeshift pestle and mortar and smiled back at Gabby, then pointed to the place where Sue had been sick and said something unintelligible.

Gabby made a cradle with her arms to show it was pregnancy sickness, wondering as she did so if these very healthy-looking people actually had such a thing.

Evidently they did. The woman smiled and nodded, then beckoned to Gabby and led her into the hut. She gestured to her to wait in the first room, went off and came back a few minutes later with a gnarled piece of root.

She indicated that Sue should chew it, and handed it to Gabby. She remembered to take it with her right hand, thanked her with a bow and smile and went back to Jed. 'A pregnant woman gave me this when I explained the problem. Do you suppose it's ginger? It looks a bit like it.'

He frowned at it, turned it this way and that and tried to break it, but it was too tough and fibrous. One of the Indonesian engineers pulled out a penknife and Jed cut into the root and sniffed, then chewed the little piece he'd removed.

'Hmm. It tastes a little different, but it's very similar.

It might be a wild form. Did she understand? I mean, it's not an abortifacient, I hope?'

Gabby shook her head. 'No, I'm sure it's not. Hang on.'

She took the root back and returned to the woman, who was pounding again. She held it out and pointed back to the hut, then pointed to her stomach and mimed retching. The woman nodded happily. Then Gabby pointed to her stomach, cradled her arms again and made a flushing away gesture with her hands to indicate losing the baby. The woman shook her head vigorously and started to talk nineteen to the dozen, miming chewing and pointing to her own distended abdomen.

Gabby nodded, sure she was now understood, and went back to the others. 'She got very agitated when I mimed losing the baby, and indicated that she'd taken it. I'm sure it's just to stop the sickness.'

'I think we could risk it, then,' Jed said slowly, and Sue waved a hand at him.

'In which case, for God's sake let's do it. I can't cope with this,' Sue muttered, and Jed cut her off a small piece and handed it to her.

After a few minutes she sighed with relief and lay down again. 'Thank God,' she said fervently.

'Better?' Jed asked.

'Much.'

'So much for drug trials,' Gabby said with a laugh. 'I'll go and thank our friend.'

The woman had finished her pounding and was sitting with a wicked-looking *parang* and chopping up strange oval fruit of some kind, prickly and olive-green. She beckoned to Gabby and patted the ground beside her.

It was cool and shady, the house behind casting a shadow just wide enough to sit in. Gabby smiled and sat down cross-legged next to her new friend and inspected the food she was preparing.

The green things looked like aubergines inside, and Gabby thought they might be jackfruit. Whatever they were, they were all cut up and put in a huge iron pot. The woman moved on to slice some lengths of what looked like young bamboo, and then some other things, the identity of which Gabby couldn't even begin to guess at. She imagined it was all edible, provided too many of those bright little chillies didn't end up in the dish!

Garlic she recognised, going into the pot with the other ingredients, and then the pot was set on some hot embers and given a stir, and the paste that had been pounded earlier was scraped into the pot. Water from a jug was poured over the top, and Gabby reckoned she'd seen her first native Indonesian vegetable stew created.

The girl then sat back on her heels, grinned at Gabby and said, '*Makan*.'

At last! An Indonesian word she had heard before! She smiled and nodded, then pointed to herself. 'Gabby,' she said. Jed was wandering across the open area and she beckoned him over. 'Jed,' she said, pointing to him, then to herself, 'Gabby.'

The girl smiled and pointed to herself. 'Gabby,' she repeated.

Gabby shook her head. 'No.' She pointed to her breasts, then to the girl's, and said, 'Woman.' Then she pointed to Jed in the region of his shorts, and said, 'Man.'

The girl giggled deliciously and covered her face with her hands. Then Gabby did the Gabby and Jed routine again, and the penny dropped.

She pointed to Gabby and repeated her name, then to Jed and repeated his, then to herself. 'Hari,' she said.

Gabby felt a grin almost split her face. 'Hari,' she

repeated, pointing at the girl, and laughed with delight. Such a simple accomplishment, to learn someone's name, but what an achievement.

She almost forgot that the girl's tribe was responsible for her capture. She pointed to the bubbling cook-pot, repeated, '*Makan*,' and turned to Jed. 'I'm learning,' she said with a grin.

His smile was indulgent. He took her arm and drew her gently to her feet, then bowed at Hari and led Gabby away from the village to the bathing pool.

'Do I smell or something?' she asked with a grin, still ridiculously pleased with herself.

He returned her grin. 'No worse than me. I wanted to talk to you out of range of the others.' He stripped off to his briefs, slid into the chilly water and beckoned to her. 'Come on, then.'

She did, only because the water looked so inviting and not because he said so. She pulled off her shoes, shirt and trousers and went into the water in her underwear. To hell with modesty—she was steaming.

'What did you want to talk to me about?' she said, once she'd got her breath back from the shock of the water.

'I want to get Derek stable, then I think we need to get him out of here. I have no idea when my e-mail will get picked up or even if it will. I'm relying on my secretary to use her initiative. She usually does, but I don't want to take her for granted. I've been sending her research results by e-mail so she may be on the lookout, but I have a horrible sinking feeling she has a week's holiday some time now.'

Gabby rolled her eyes. 'Great. Isn't there anyone else?'

He gave a shrug. 'Not offhand. I don't suppose you know anyone's e-mail number?'

'By heart?' She shook her head. 'No. I've tried, but I can't think of anyone. I'm not really a computery sort of person.'

He tutted at her and she poked her tongue out at him and lay back in the water. 'Just imagine, these people live here without any of these so-called necessities, eking out their simple existence by gathering food from the forest—'

'Nature's bountiful harvest?' Jed said with a little snort. 'They're riddled with parasites, plagued by malaria and filariasis, dysentery and malnutrition. They have no health service, no surgery, no antenatal care, dentists don't exist—'

'But if they don't eat refined sugars they probably don't need dentists,' Gabby reasoned. 'And, anyway, it's probably better than dying of stress-related illnesses like we do in the West. I'm sure they have all sorts of herbal remedies that are very effective—probably some of them even more effective than the ones we've come to rely on. You can bet your life no Indonesian village in the mountains is plagued by the MRSA bug!'

He laughed. 'You're just an optimist. You wait till you get sick and see what you want, western medicine or Indonesian *jamu*.'

She sobered, thinking of Derek for whom the Indonesians would have no treatment. 'How's Derek's blood sugar?' she asked.

'Coming down. It's still a little high, but I want to get the last bit down gradually. He's all right now, just a little queasy, but that's natural. I've given him some of Hari's ginger, too. It seemed to help a little.' He climbed out of the pool and sat on the rocks by the side, dripping all over the stone and giving Gabby altogether too much to look at.

'I want to have a meeting with the priest,' he was

saying. 'He seems to be the doctor as well, and I might be able to impress on him the need to have us released. I also want to tell them about the grave trees and ask if they're the reason, but without language it's a little tricky. I don't suppose you can draw?'

'Me?' She shrugged. 'A little—but do we have any paper?'

'Derek brought some, and a pen. We could try drawing the lake and the trees, and see if we get a reaction—'

Something flew low over his head and he ducked, flinging his arms up instinctively and losing his balance so he fell back into the water. When he came up Gabby was laughing. 'Well, that certainly got a reaction,' she choked.

He was at her side in two lazy strokes, and pushed her under the water. She came up spluttering and fighting, her fists connecting with his chest and her legs tangling with his, so that she could feel—

'Oh,' she said softly, her eyes widening with surprise.

He stared into her eyes for an age, then his head lowered and his mouth brushed hers. 'Gabby, I want you,' he said softly, 'but it isn't going to happen. There's too much else going on—we need to keep our heads clear.'

She pushed away from him, treading water while their eyes locked, and then with a sigh she turned and swam to the edge and climbed out. 'Fine,' she said in a choked voice. 'Just stop getting me alone and winding me up and it'll be easy.'

She pulled on her clothes and left him there in the water, cooling off. Do him good. Who did he think he was talking to? So he wanted her, did he?

And she wanted him. She bit back a little moan of frustration and stomped back towards the clearing. She saw a shadow above her, and ducked from another of the swooping whatevers, glanced over her shoulder and then suppressed a shriek.

A bat nearly two feet across?

She headed back to the hut almost at a run, and went up the ladder and into the relative sanctuary of the dimly lit interior like a rat out of a trap.

'Hi, folks!' she said brightly, and plopped down on a heap of folded bedding near Derek. He was lounging against a post, looking better than he had at breakfast and infinitely more human than he had the night before, and she considered again the miracle of modern medicine while her heart settled down again.

'How are you feeling?' she asked him, sure of what the answer would be.

He smiled wanly. 'Almost back to normal, thanks to you two. I'm sorry you got dragged into this mess.'

Gabby grinned. 'Actually, daft though it might seem, I'm almost enjoying myself. It's an opportunity to see an untouched culture and get to know a genuinely friendly people—'

'Very friendly,' Jed said drily, entering the hut behind her. 'So friendly they insist on you coming to stay with them.'

She swivelled round and fixed him with a look. 'We want to desecrate the graves of their children,' she said very slowly and clearly. 'I think they have a right to be a little bit antsy about it!'

'There are ways of communicating—'

'By e-mail?' she said sweetly. 'Anyway, talking of communication, I thought you were going to have a chat to the doctor-priest fellow.'

'I am. I want you to come too. Let's scrounge up some paper and go to it.'

She got reluctantly to her feet and did as he suggested, then they went out and stood at the bottom of the ladder and looked around. 'OK, so which one is he?' Gabby asked.

Jed shrugged. 'Let's ask your friend, Hari.'

She was busy parcelling up little pieces of some indeterminate meat in leaves and burying them in the ashes around the pot as they approached her. She sat back on her heels and gave them her lovely smile.

'Gabby,' she said.

Gabby smiled. 'Hello, Hari.' She squatted down beside the woman and waved a questioning hand at the village. 'Doctor?' she said hopefully.

Hari looked puzzled so Jed crouched down too and pointed at himself. 'Jed, doctor,' he told her. '*Obat—jamu—dukun.*'

'*Dukun!*' Hari exclaimed, and broke into a torrent of her unintelligible native tongue.

'What's a *dukun*?' Gabby asked Jed.

'An Indonesian folk-doctor—like a sort of witch-doctor with an amazing battery of natural remedies. Some of them are quacks, but some are fantastic. Your friend seems to be getting very excited so we might be in luck.'

'Hari, is there a *dukun*?' Gabby asked, pointing round the village.

She scrambled to her feet, wiped her hands on her skirt and led them over to a hut. Gesturing to them to wait, she approached a gnarled old man sitting in the shade under the ladder, fanning himself with a huge leaf.

She spoke to him rapidly, waving at Gabby and Jed, and then the old man stood up and drew himself to his full height.

He reached almost to Gabby's chin, and he was dressed like all the other men in a hammered bark loin-cloth and tattoos. He had a gleaming white bone through his nose and ash over his dark, withered skin, and he looked ancient. His eyes, however, were like polished conkers, bright and lively and incongruous in so lined and venerable a face.

He looked only at Jed, giving Gabby a cursory once-over and dismissing her. Taking Jed's arm, he led him under the hut into the shade and they sat down cross-legged. Gabby, standing in the full sun, began to wonder about the natural order of things that dictated that women toiled in the sun while men sat in the shade, smoked their evil clove cigarettes and drank out of tubes of bamboo.

Perhaps there were things about this wonderful and untouched culture that weren't quite perfect!

Jed caught her eye and winked, and she smiled sweetly and stood there until he beckoned her.

'Draw the lake and the trees for him. I've tried and I can't do it well enough. I don't think they're exposed enough to 2-D images to understand.'

She tried not to smile at his efforts. Art was obviously not his forte, but one couldn't be good at everything and he was a hell of a kisser...

She dragged her mind back to the subject at hand and thought for a moment, then tried to recreate the scene from memory. As she drew the trees and put the squares on the trunks the old man seemed to become very agitated, and when she drew a baby and pointed from the baby to the tree he nodded vigorously.

Then she drew the trees cut down and lying on their sides and a building in their place, and he got very angry and started to mutter and chant.

Gabby touched his arm gently, took the page and screwed it up then put it into Hari's fire. When she returned he was looking puzzled. She drew the scene again, extended the river and drew the power station at a different site. She didn't know where she'd drawn it, and just hoped it wasn't on the site of some other burial ground or sacred spot.

Obviously it wasn't. He stared at the paper for a long while, turned it this way and that and then took the paper, folded it and tucked it into his loincloth. He turned away, and Hari touched them on the arm and beckoned them away, indicating that their audience was over.

'I suppose that means he's going to think about it,' Jed said drily as they walked back to their hut.

'He'll probably do what an Anglican priest would do and pray over it, only I expect he'll sacrifice something and wait for the gods to tell him the way forward. Not so very different.'

'At least he seemed to understand the drawing.'

'By a miracle. I thought he was going to have us killed when I cut the trees down and put the power station there.'

Jed laughed softly. 'You and me both. That might have been a little rash.'

'It told us what we needed to know, though. It *is* the trees that are the problem. I should add an addendum to your e-mail.'

'For all the good it'll do us.' He sighed and sat down in the shade near the hut. 'I wonder what's for lunch? It seems a long time since we had that fruit for breakfast.'

'I wonder what the meat was in those parcels?' she said speculatively.

'Don't ask,' Jed advised sagely. 'Probably bat or monkey.'

She shuddered. 'Just as long as it isn't snake or frogs, I don't care.'

He laughed. 'I remember listening to a radio programme about some scientists who were taken hostage on Irian Jaya. They said that rat was tough, pig was fatty but the frogs were delicious.'

Gabby gave him a sceptical look, firmly unconvinced. 'How many of them died?' she asked drily.

'None from food poisoning. I think if the natives eat it we can assume it's safe for us to, but we need to boil water for teeth and drinking unless we stick to coconut milk and *tuak*. Rather nice stuff, that. The *dukun* gave me some.'

'I saw you drinking away with him,' she sniped, remembering being left out in the sun. 'Was it nice and cool?'

'What's the matter—didn't you like standing in the background, being servile?'

She threw a bit of twig at him and laughed. 'Tell me about this *tuak*. What is it?'

'Palm wine. They tap the sap from a palm tree and pour it into lengths of bamboo and seal it for a day or so. It ferments naturally and gives a lovely warm glow.' He grinned. 'A sort of naturally occurring gin and tonic without the quinine.'

'No doubt you'll have to research it heavily,' she said innocently.

'Oh, of course. Perhaps you can persuade your friend, Hari, to show you how to make it for me as befits your station. After all, you are supposed to be my wife.'

She snorted. 'Don't hold your breath. My acting skills aren't that brilliant.' She doodled in the sand. 'So, anyway, now they know we know about the trees, do you think they'll let us go?'

He shrugged. 'Depends on what the gods tell our friend, I guess. Maybe, maybe not. We'll have to play it by ear. I wouldn't hold your breath, though, we could still be here for weeks. What we need, of course,' he continued after a pause, 'is an interpreter—some way of communicating with them. We could also do with having a chance to talk to Bill about the possibility of re-siting the power station.'

'I wouldn't have thought he could refuse—not with seven lives at stake,' Gabby pointed out, but Jed shrugged again.

'The Indonesian government gave him consent and passed all the plans. He's got permission for his holiday resort because he was going to provide free electricity to Telok Panjang. At the moment it struggles on kerosene and the odd generator, and the government obviously thought it were getting a good deal. They may decide to throw their weight behind Bill and send troops in to deal with this little insurrection.'

'And we'll all get caught in the crossfire. Great.' Gabby stood up. 'I want to go for a walk around the village.'

'To see if you can find a way out?' Jed said wryly.

'Oh, yeah. Absolutely.'

He stood up and brushed the dirt off his trousers. 'I'll come. Your friend still seems to be watching you so I'd be careful about being alone anywhere too isolated.'

They wandered down to the mountain pool where they had swum that morning and turned left, following the river downhill for a while. There was a path which was quite well used, and it crossed others, a veritable network of tracks and trails that criss-crossed the area around the village.

They wove through them, keeping an ear out all the time for the sounds of children playing and making sure they didn't go too far.

Not that it would have mattered. They were followed at a discreet distance by a gang of little children, tittering and squeaking like a litter of baby mice. They pretended to ignore them, and looked around at the forest.

One tree caught Gabby's attention because of its strange structure. It had a network of stems stretching up in a circle around a hollow core, as if the tree had grown up like a fungus from a ring of roots, and the children were playing hide and seek inside it.

'It's a strangler fig,' Jed told her. 'They germinate halfway up one of the forest trees, send down aerial roots to the soil and then continue to grow upwards. Eventually they link up with each other in a band and strangle the host tree, which dies and rots down to provide nourishment for the growing fig trees. It's probably several trees, not just one. Look, there are figs on it.'

There were, but she shunned them, mindful of the effect they might have. They continued on their way, circling the village until they were almost back, then suddenly the children vanished and an eerie silence descended.

A chill ran over Gabby, and she moved instinctively closer to Jed. 'Everything's gone quiet,' she whispered. 'Even the monkeys are quiet.'

He pointed ahead of them at a tree, and there in the trunk she saw a number of neat, square patches on the bark. Most had started to heal but there was one, though, that was unhealed, indicating a grave tree in current use and, judging by the look of it, used very recently.

She closed her eyes and a tear slipped out. 'Oh, Jed,' she said and, turning, she buried her head in his chest and sobbed.

'Hey, softy, it's a fact of life,' he told her gently.

'I know,' she mumbled, wiping her eyes on his soggy shirtfront. 'I'm just being silly. It's because they're babies, and there seem to be so many little holes for so few people. They must lose their babies all the time.'

'Perhaps that's why the children that are still alive are

strong and healthy—perhaps nature sorts them out early so that only the really tough ones make it.'

She sniffed and straightened up. 'Don't be logical,' she told him, and with a last lingering look at the quiet glade with its sad little secrets she turned away and carried on with her walk.

Jed fell into step beside her. 'If you get so emotional and weepy about a few babies you've never met, how on earth do you cope with losing a child you've nursed?'

She gave a humourless grunt of laughter. 'Badly,' she told him with characteristic honesty. 'Usually I fall apart afterwards, but I have been known to cry at the time more often than I care to remember.'

'How did I know that?' he murmured and, slinging his arm around her shoulders, he gave her a quick squeeze. 'Come on, my stomach tells me it must be lunchtime. Let's go and find out what that meat was that Hari was putting in the fire.'

'If it's fruit bat I'm not eating it,' she warned, and he laughed.

'You could get awfully thin in the next few days.'

'So be it,' she said firmly. 'But I'm not eating bats for anybody!'

They walked back into the clearing arm in arm and laughing, to find two men on their knees in the middle of the open ground. A cluster of what looked like village elders stood around them with spears pointing menacingly at them, and at their head was the *dukun* in full ceremonial dress, chanting tunelessly.

'Damn,' Jed said softly.

'What?'

'It's Jamal and his friend Johannis, the man who's an outcast from this village.'

'Isn't that good?'

Jed looked from the group to her and back to the

group. 'I somehow don't think so,' he said softly. 'I think, if they aren't about to kill them, we've just got ourselves two more fellow-hostages.'

And with that he strode into the middle of the group of men, stood in front of the *dukun* and began, so Gabby imagined, to intercede.

CHAPTER SEVEN

'HE's off his trolley,' Sue said quietly, appearing at Gabby's elbow. 'Come into the hut out of the way—it could get nasty.'

Gabby needed no second bidding. She'd always thought Jed was a bit of an Indiana Jones, but surely he didn't have to take it quite so seriously? She followed Sue up the ladder and sat, watching anxiously from just inside the doorway through a crack in the bark-covered wall.

Jamal and his friend stayed where they were, but she noticed that Jed was speaking to the other man, who was in turn speaking to the *dukun* and relaying messages back.

The conversation was inaudible, but after a moment the *dukun* waved away the men with their spears and told Jamal and Johannis to get up. They were then led to a hut and thrown in, and a guard was posted outside the door.

Then the *dukun* waved his spear at Hari, who was standing on the fringe, and went back to his shady spot under his hut. The elders with their spears stood, looking disgruntled, for a moment, then turned away and shuffled back to their business, and Jed was left standing there in the middle alone.

After a second they saw him shrug and make his way towards them. Hari was serving food to the *dukun*, and nobody seemed to make any attempt to stop Jed. Within seconds he was up the ladder and they all pounced on him.

'Well?' Sue said impatiently. 'Are there others behind them? Are we going to be rescued?'

Jed sighed and shook his head. 'No. The elders were going to kill them, but I managed to persuade the *dukun* to spare them so we can use them as interpreters to negotiate between us and the tribe and the Indonesian government and Bill. I said it would be a terrible tragedy if they were unable to communicate their concerns and the trees were destroyed, without proper respect being shown for the burial site.'

'Crafty thing,' Derek said with a chuckle. 'I thought you'd had your chips, Jed. I thought for sure you were going to bite the dust back there.'

Jed gave a quirky little grin. '*You* thought that? How do you think *I* felt!'

Hari appeared in the doorway with a huge wooden platter laden with food, and passed it in to them. She gave Gabby a shy smile, bobbed her head at Jed as if he were some kind of spirit and backed away again.

'Great,' he said, reaching for one of the charred little leaf parcels they had seen being put on the fire. 'Let's see if it's rat or bat.'

Sue groaned, turned away and reached for another little piece of the ginger root. 'Jed, you are foul,' she muttered and, turning her back on them all, she chewed her way back to equilibrium.

If Gabby had thought the arrival of Jamal and Johannis signalled a change in their circumstances she was wrong. The days seemed to drag by with more of the same nothingness, and after a week everyone was getting crabby and difficult.

Every night Jed checked the Magellan instrument to see if he'd had a reply and every night he sighed, switched it off and put it away as their hopes crumbled in the dust.

He tried to talk the *dukun* into letting Jamal go back to Telok Panjang but he wouldn't hear of it, presumably because it would give away their whereabouts. The men were guarded night and day, although Jed seemed to be allowed to go and talk to them, and he discovered that everyone was convinced they had all been murdered.

Penny had been sent back to Jakarta as planned, he told them all, and Jon, a government official and Bill Freeman, the developer, were in endless meetings. At least they had been. By now they might have decided to track the tribe down but, since Johannis was the only man to know the way, it seemed unlikely they would be discovered.

Gabby found the waiting very difficult, and passed the time as well as possible by making friends. She spent time with Hari, getting to know her in a strangely silent way, and by observing her carefully through the days she realised Hari was very tired and uncomfortable, although she never complained.

She spoke to Jed about it one night, carefully separated by a foot of floor and maintaining a strict rule of no physical contact through the night. It was less frustrating that way, they'd discovered, and by an unspoken agreement had settled into the companionable but slightly distant routine.

Tonight, though, she didn't want to be distant. She rolled on her side to face him, pillowing her head on her arm, and tapped his shoulder to get his attention.

'Mmm?' he murmured drowsily.

'It's about Hari,' she said softly. 'She's huge and she doesn't seem to be showing any signs of going into labour, but she's very uncomfortable. Today she was really bad.'

His eyes flickered open in the half-dark. 'Yes, I'd noticed. I wonder if she's got a breech? It might not be triggering her uterus to contract if so, or just feebly.'

'So what will happen?'

'Nothing until it's too late, then weak contractions that get nowhere. She might have an antepartum haemorrhage and die, or the baby might turn and everything will be all right, or she might go into very strong labour and rupture her uterus and die that way. Or she might just work like stink and get away with it if there are enough people to help her who know what they're doing.'

'Like us?' Gabby suggested.

'Forget it,' he told her. 'Even if we could get near her, what could we do?'

Gabby rolled onto her front and propped herself up on her elbows, her head close to his so they could hear each other without disturbing the others. 'We have to do something, Jed. We can't just ignore her, can we? Surely we can do something?'

He snorted. 'How? We haven't got access to any diagnostic tools, we can't scan her or X-ray her or even examine her. I don't suppose for a moment I'd be allowed to perform an internal on a young pregnant woman, do you? Think about it. I bet the only birth attendants will be the older women—and the *dukun* if things get really bad. No way will they let me in there.'

'How about me?' she suggested.

'More likely, but still not very probable. It depends how desperate they get. Of course Jamal thinks you're a healer so that could work in our favour. I'll talk to him in the morning.'

He didn't get a chance, though, because they were woken later that night by a woman's screams.

Gabby leapt up instantly. 'Hari,' she said with conviction. 'Jed, I want to go to her.'

'Try getting dressed first, then,' he suggested, stopping her in her tracks.

Bemused, she turned back and pulled on her clothes in place of the sarong, freezing as the air was ripped again by another cry. A shiver ran down her spine. 'Jed, please come too. If they let me in I can perhaps talk to you through the wall, but something's dreadfully wrong. Women don't scream like that normally.'

'God, I haven't done obstetrics since I was twenty-seven—I doubt if I can remember what's what,' he muttered.

'Let's just hope you're better with obstetrics than you are with e-mail numbers, then, or I might be better off without you.'

'Ha-ha,' he growled, dragging on his trousers and following her out of the hut.

The action was all taking place in and around Hari's hut, they discovered. Her husband, a strong and healthy-looking young man, was sitting at the fire with another man, whom they recognised as the chief, smoking clove cigarettes and talking in muttered undertones.

'You know Hari is the chief's daughter, do you?' Jed murmured as they approached.

'Yes, I'd gathered. That must be why he's here. I wonder where the *dukun* is.'

'Inside, I expect, chanting and giving her ghastly potions. I should think he's given her something to speed up the contractions, hence the screams.'

'Don't,' Gabby said with a shudder. 'How am I going to get inside?'

'Just go in. You're a woman. If you're humble enough they might let you help. I'll see if I can talk them into letting Johannis out to interpret.'

She climbed the ladder and slipped into the hut un-
noticed, and found everyone clustered round Hari who
was lying on the floor, writhing. Everyone in the room
was a woman, with the exception of the *dukun*, who was
squatting beside her chanting as Jed had predicted.

He looked up at her and stopped, then pointed at the
door and said something that was obviously telling her
to leave. She shook her head and knelt down on the other
side of Hari, facing him, and pointed to herself. 'Gabby,
dukun,' she said, hoping he would believe her and enlist
her aid, or at least allow her to help.

Would he feel threatened, as if his magic was no
good?

He sat back on his heels, folded his arms and stared
at her defiantly—challengingly. Gabby swallowed and
bent over Hari, stroking her hair back from her face and
murmuring soothingly to her.

A woman pressed a damp cloth into her hand and she
used that, wiping away the beads of sweat on Hari's
clammy skin. 'Hari? Hari, it's Gabby,' she told her, and
the girl's eyes flickered open.

They were glazed with pain and fear, and she clutched
Gabby's hand and began to weep silently. Gabby used
the other hand and laid it on the hugely distended abdomen, palpating it thoughtfully. It was years since she'd
done much obstetrics, but she knew that what she was
feeling now wasn't run of the mill.

For a start, she realised with a shock as she palpated
the edges of the woman's abdomen, Hari was having
twins, and—if she wasn't very much mistaken—it was
a double transverse lie, one baby in the lap of the other,
both crosswise.

'Gabby?'

She lifted her head at Jed's voice. 'She's having

twins—a double transverse presentation. Jed, she doesn't stand a chance without a section.'

He swore, softly but succinctly, and called to her to come out. 'Johannis is here, he can interpret. We've been talking to the husband. Apparently she's been in labour for a day off and on, without complaining, but she's starting to have much stronger contractions.'

'I can tell,' she called, her hand still resting where it was. There was suddenly a tremendous tension under her palm, and Hari cried out and rolled up into a ball, tensing all her muscles.

Gabby stroked her back soothingly, talking reassuringly to her, and when the contraction was over she slipped out of the hut and went to see Jed. 'Her contractions are horrendously strong, and she's never going to make any progress. Jed, she's going to die unless we can operate.'

Jed stabbed his hands through his hair and looked up at the sky for inspiration. 'I can't, Gabby. There's no anaesthetic, no light, no after-care—she'd die anyway, and if we've interfered we'll probably die too.'

'So you're just going to leave her to it?' she said furiously. 'Jed, you can't. We can do it—surely you've got some painkillers in that box of tricks.'

He snorted. 'Nothing that strong. I've got a couple of phials of pethidine, that's all, and no antibiotics strong enough to dare risk it, not in these unsterile conditions.'

She twisted her hands together worriedly. 'There must be something we can do.'

'Only if the *dukun* has a narcotic available in his arsenal of natural remedies, and he might well have—and if he's prepared to help us, which he might not be.'

'Ask—get Johannis to tell the chief his daughter's going to die unless we help her. Get him to tell the man that we're healers too. Get him to order the *dukun* to help.'

'Just like that?' He shook his head in despair and turned to Johannis, and explained the situation to him through Jamal.

'Wah,' the man said, rolling his eyes in fear and starting to babble.

'I think what he means is he can't tell the chief that because he'll cut his head off,' Jed translated.

'I'll cut his head off—Johannis, please, tell the chief his daughter's dying,' she pleaded.

Just then another scream cut through the night, and the chief looked anxiously at the hut. Gabby, not one to hang about in the face of such an emergency, pushed Johannis over to the fireside. 'Tell him,' she snarled.

So the poor man, shaking and trembling, translated their message. The chief's eyes widened in fear, then glazed and filled and he started to sob. The husband fell on him and they wept together.

'Oh, this is hopeless,' Gabby said impatiently, and pulled the two men apart. 'Jed, *dukun*,' she told them firmly. 'Hari...' She pulled her finger over her throat. 'Jed help.'

They looked at her as if she were mad. 'Johannis,' she wailed, and he spoke again. She turned to Jed. 'Make sure he tells them about the operation.'

There was a muttered exchange between Jed, Jamal and Johannis, and then their intrepid translator tried again. This time the chief got to his feet and went to the door of the hut and called out.

The *dukun* appeared in the doorway and they had a brief, fierce exchange. Jed got Johannis to translate, and then relayed it to Gabby.

'The *dukun* doesn't want to help us. He's now admitted he can't do anything and, yes, she will die.'

At this the chief produced a knife and threatened the man.

'Things are hotting up—he might be on our side,' Jed muttered to Gabby, rubbing thoughtfully at the beard on his chin. He turned to Johannis and said something which the man then translated, and the *dukun* nodded, his face surly.

'I don't think he wants to help, but on the other hand I think he's quite happy being alive. The chief's just told him that if Hari dies he dies too.'

'So I guess the same will apply to us.'

Jed grinned at her. 'I love a challenge. We need to scrub, kiddo. I think we're about to do surgery al fresco style, and the anaesthetist has got a serious case of the sulks.'

Adrenaline, Gabby thought some half an hour later, was a wonderful thing. Talk about sharpening up your wits!

Hari had been washed and sedated with the *dukun*'s herbal remedy, and was now sleeping peacefully in her hut. The women had been herded out, only the woman's mother, the *dukun*, Jed and Gabby remaining, with Johannis outside the door to translate if necessary.

They had scrubbed as well as they could and sprayed their hands with antibiotic spray, and Jed used more of it to sterilise the incision site. 'I'll do a longitudinal section because I don't want to cut the babies, and this light's awful. Anyway, it's quicker and she's less likely to have problems later with another delivery.'

He picked up the knife he'd been given by their reluctant assistant and which he'd sterilised as well as possible by boiling it in water for ten minutes. 'Let's hope this sedation works,' he said to Gabby, and without further ado he ran the knife down the skin.

A thin beading of blood appeared along the line, and

Hari moaned and moved a little. Her mother soothed her with trembling hands, tears streaming silently down her wrinkled face, and Jed stroked again and again until he was through the muscle layer and the uterus was revealed.

'It's very thinned at the base—I think it would have ruptured within another hour or so. I wish I could do an ultrasound scan to find out where the placentas are,' he muttered. 'Let's just pray I don't hit one of them.'

He stroked the knife over the uterus, pierced it and then, by sliding his fingers under the knife the wrong way up, he opened the uterus far enough to reveal the babies.

'So far so good. Right, let's see what we've got here.'

'Wah!' the mother keened softly as Jed reached in and lifted the first tiny infant out. It squalled healthily, and he grinned and handed it to Gabby. She laid it on Hari's chest and waited for the second child. It wasn't long coming, and also squalled vigorously.

Jed turned to Johannis and asked something, which was relayed to the astonished *dukun*. He reached in his bag of potions and produced a root, which he slivered with a knife and handed to Hari's mother with an instruction.

She placed it under Hari's tongue, and a few minutes later the uterus contracted steadily and the placentas came naturally away.

'Well, I never. Oxytocin, as I live and breathe.'

Jed smiled grimly. 'So far so good. Right, let's separate these babies from their placentas, take them out and get her closed up before too many moths fall inside.'

He closed quickly, more quickly than Gabby had ever seen it done and probably nearly as neatly, using the antibiotic spray liberally as he went along. Then he cleaned up his hands, washed the site down and sprayed

it again, before covering it with a non-adherent sterile
dressing.

Then he sat back on his heels and looked at Gabby.

'Well? What have we got?'

'Two boys, both well and fit and hungry. I don't suppose he's got a natural antidote to that sedative so she
can feed them?'

Jed laughed. 'I think we'd better let her sleep it off,'
he said. 'The longer she's out of it the better. I'm sure
another woman can be persuaded into service as a wet
nurse.'

He spoke to Johannis, then turned to the *dukun* and
held out his hand with a grin.

After a few seconds' hesitation he took it and smiled,
and said something to Johannis who translated.

Jed relayed it back to Gabby. 'He says together we
have powerful magic,' he said with a grin. 'I reckon we
were just damned lucky.'

'So far,' Gabby agreed, looking at the sleeping woman
who had been all but unaware of the procedure. 'Never
mind the magic—thank goodness he had a powerful
enough painkiller. Let's just pray she doesn't get an infection.'

'I'm sure our friend here has something as impressive
in the way of a natural antibiotic. I'd make up a garlic
paste dressing and lay it on if all else failed, but he's
probably got a whole battery of goodies up his sleeve.'

He stood up, moved to Hari's head and squatted down
by her mother, who was cradling the babies in her arms.
They were both squalling furiously, and were quite obviously well and healthy. They were very certainly alive,
at least.

Jed smiled at the woman who smiled back tearfully
and hugged the babies even tighter, then she struggled
to her feet and went over to the doorway, holding the

babies up. There was a cheer from outside and she turned back to the *dukun*, obviously thanking him for his part.

He bowed graciously, then began chanting over Hari and the babies, sprinkling them with something from his bag. 'Doubtless thanking some powerful god for the safe deliverance not only of the babies and their mother but also himself,' Jed murmured to Gabby.

She laughed softly. 'And us. I think I might join in.'

Jed hugged her, dropping a quick kiss in her hair, and together they left the hut to the greetings of the women who were still waiting for a proper look at the babies.

They were led to the fire by the happy, laughing throng and asked to sit with the chief and Hari's husband, and they were brought strong, sickly coffee and even sicklier cakes made of palm syrup in order to celebrate.

The *dukun* came out about half an hour later, smiling and bearing the babies in his arms, and they were handed to the women, who immediately took charge.

'They'll be fed and washed and looked after now,' Jed said confidently. 'The Indonesians are wonderful with children. If parents die the children are always instantly absorbed into another part of the family, and they often seem almost to share their children. I'm quite sure those babies will be fine now.'

'And Hari?'

Jed turned and spoke to Johannis who was squatting on the fringe of the group, waiting to be asked to translate again, and after a brief discussion with the *dukun* he relayed that Hari was fine and sleeping peacefully.

'Should I stay with her?' Gabby asked.

'Perhaps we all should. I don't think he would, but the *dukun* has the power, I'm quite sure, to kill her and have the blame fixed on us. I think this guy is OK, but a lot of these healers are quacks and totally unscrupulous, and they'd stop at nothing to protect their own reputations.'

'Even murder?' Gabby murmured.

'Possibly. I think, just to be on the safe side, he should have an audience at all times and, anyway, I'd rather be near Hari just until she comes round.'

In the end they stayed up by the fire until the sky began to lighten, popping in and out of the hut every few minutes to see the sleeping woman and her relieved mother. Both were fine, and after a while Hari stirred and moaned a little. The *dukun* gave her a potion which quietened her, without sedating her, and Gabby and Jed were both happy with her condition as far as they could tell.

The babies, too, were cuddled and admired once they had been fed, and they were passed around the group at the fireside with pride.

Gabby held one and Jed the other, and Gabby felt a huge lump in her throat.

'I'm so glad they didn't end up in a tree,' she said and, without thinking, she held the baby tight against her and closed her eyes.

When she opened them and looked up at Jed, his eyes seemed very bright in the firelight. He took the baby from her and passed it on, then took Gabby by the hand and led her back to their hut.

'I think she'll be all right now,' he told her and, leading her along to their bedroom, he turned her into his arms and held her tight. 'Thank you for making me do that,' he mumbled into her hair. 'I really didn't want to but, you're right, she would have died. I just thought we were bound to kill her.'

'And we didn't. I just couldn't bear to see her die, she's such a lovely person.'

'So are you,' he murmured, and his lips closed over hers. Her tiredness was forgotten, the drama of the night behind her, and only she and Jed existed.

They lay down without a sound on the scattered bedding, and Jed undressed her with trembling fingers. Everywhere he touched her skin it turned to fire, and by the time she was naked she was shaking all over.

Her fingers didn't work, and he dragged his shirt over his head, ripped off his trousers and briefs and settled beside her with a tiny sigh.

'I love you, Gabrielle Andrews,' he murmured. 'You're my little angel, do you know that? I've wanted to hold you like this for so long...'

His mouth found hers, teasing and tormenting until she thought she'd go crazy for him. His hands moved over her, cupping and cradling and stroking, making her weak with longing. She searched his body, her own hands restlessly fluttering over his back, over the skin that was like hot, damp silk in the tropic dawn. So hot, lit with the fire that was consuming them both. Amazing that he could feel so hot—

He shifted slightly and her hand found its way around and down, cupping the heavy fullness of his masculinity, dragging a groan from deep inside him.

His own hand responded, stroking the damp nest of curls that hid such a wild need she thought she'd die of it.

'Jed, please,' she whispered, and then he shifted across her and buried himself deep inside her.

She couldn't hold back the cry, couldn't help the little sob of relief at being part of him at last. He dropped his head against her shoulder with a shudder, and was still for an endless moment.

Then he lifted his head and met her eyes in the pale

light of dawn. 'Oh, Gabby,' he breathed raggedly. 'It feels so right—it's like coming home.'

Tears filled her eyes and she blinked them away, anxious to see his face—to remember every moment of this precious union. 'Jed, I love you,' she whispered.

'Oh, angel, I love you, too, so very much.'

His lips touched her face like the wing of a bird, soft, open-mouthed kisses that left a trail of fire over her eyes, her nose, her jaw, and finally her lips.

Their mouths went wild then, hungry and demanding, clinging fiercely and searching as their bodies rose to meet each other and the relentless passion broke in a devastating climax that left them both weak and shaken.

Jed collapsed against her, his breath scorching against her neck.

'God, my head aches,' he murmured a few moments later, and then his body slumped bonelessly onto hers.

'Jed—Jed, get off, I can't breathe,' she whispered.

There was silence, broken only by the harsh rasp of his breathing, and it dawned on Gabby that something was horribly wrong...

CHAPTER EIGHT

'JED?'

He was heavy on her, so heavy she could hardly roll him off. She pushed him, hissed at him, shook him, all to no avail. He seemed oblivious to her, and now that the wild heat of passion had cooled in her Gabby could feel that the heat coming off him in waves was far from normal.

In fact, it was worryingly abnormal, coupled with his lack of reaction and the headache he'd spoken of. Now he seemed to be unconscious, his body shaking violently.

She gave a mighty heave and rolled his shuddering body off her, then knelt beside him. 'Jed? Talk to me, damn it!'

He mumbled something unintelligible and curled into a ball, hugging his arms around himself as if he was cold, and Gabby covered him with one of the loosely woven rugs, pulled on her clothes and went out to see the others. There was a deep chill of fear settling round her heart, and she needed Jed's advice.

Unfortunately he wasn't in a position to give it to her.

She found the others grouped round in the living area by the door, eating their breakfast. Conversation stopped dead as she walked in, and she realised that in the flimsy hut their love-making had probably been quite clearly audible.

Tough. She had other things to worry about.

'Have any of you ever seen cerebral malaria?' she asked them.

132

'I have,' Ismail said.

'I don't suppose you'd recognise it?'

'Jed?' Sue asked her, the curiosity on her face replaced by concern.

'I think so. He complained of a headache, and he's burning up and shivering and I can't seem to get through to him. He might just be very tired, but I don't think so.'

Sue was on her feet in an instant, following Gabby back to their bedroom, with Ismail behind her and the others trailing at a distance.

Jed was pale and sweaty, his sunken eyes shadowed in his bearded face. 'He looks awful,' Sue said bluntly, and knelt down beside him. 'Jed? Come on, wake up!'

He mumbled something and stirred, but his eyes didn't open and he didn't really respond.

'He's out of it—how long has he been like this?'

Gabby shrugged. How long was it? 'Twenty minutes? Half an hour? Not that long.'

'Looks bad, mem,' Ismail said, squatting down beside him and touching his hot skin with a tentative hand. 'My cousin died—'

'Thank you, Ismail, we can manage now,' Sue said quickly, but Gabby felt a chill run right through her.

'You don't suppose it could just be flu, do you?' she asked, knowing as she did so that she was clutching at straws.

'No. I think it's almost certainly malaria. There's a leaflet about treating all the different types in the medicines he brought with him, and I'm sure he would have brought the right things to treat it. We just have to get the drugs into him.'

And that, Gabby knew, would be almost impossible without his co-operation or an intravenous drip. She found the flight bag, dug about in it for the leaflet and then read it quickly.

'"Severe headache, fever, drowsiness, delirium or confusion may indicate impending cerebral malaria",' she read aloud. 'Blah blah—"chloroquine-resistant strains—quinine, pyrimethamine and a sulphonamide orally, or chloroquine dihydrochloride IV if unconscious".'

She looked up at Sue. 'I would say he's unconscious. I think I ought to try injecting him very slowly intravenously, just to get something into him, and then try orally as soon as he comes round a bit or we can get him to co-operate. Will you help me?'

'Of course. What do you want me to do?'

And that was the problem, of course. There was nothing she could do except provide moral support, and Gabby said so. 'Just stay with me. I'm so scared he'll die…'

She dropped her face into her hands and choked down a sob, then lifted her head, took a deep breath and dredged up a smile. She had to think—

'OK. The first hurdle is saline solution. There isn't any.'

'You'll have to use boiled water.'

Gabby rolled her eyes. 'I could be giving him God knows what. OK, I'll use boiled water. Could you organise some?'

While Sue went in search of boiled water in something reasonably sterile, Gabby read and reread the leaflet until she was sure she'd understood the treatment, then she looked through the medicines and found everything she needed.

'Thank God he brought it,' she muttered, and looked up just as Sue came back with not only a bowl of water but the *dukun* in tow.

She wasn't sure if she was relieved to see him or not, but he might have some magic cure up his sleeve that wouldn't hurt as adjuvant therapy, and just now Gabby would settle for all the help she could get!

He squatted down by Jed's head, laid a hand on his scorching forehead and then pulled up his eyelids. Jed moaned a little, and the old man shook his head slightly and turned to Gabby, pointing to his head and holding it as if in pain.

She nodded, and hugged her arms around herself to show he had been shivery, and then fanned her face to show he was hot.

The old man unfolded himself and disappeared, presumably to fetch something. Gabby watched him go, and turned back to Sue. 'Did you ask him to come?'

'No. He just followed me. I had to talk to Johannis to get him to explain what I wanted, and he must have got wind of it. I wonder what he's gone to get.'

'Hopefully Johannis, amongst other things, so we can have an intelligent conversation. Could you hold his arm for me?'

She pulled up some of the water in the syringe, prayed that it was all right and drew up the chloroquine. Then she tied Jed's belt around his arm to raise the vein, slid the needle in and checked she'd entered the vein, then released the belt. Then gradually, millilitre by millilitre, she squeezed the contents of the syringe into his arm.

She was about halfway through when the *dukun* came back, and he watched her impassively as she delivered the drug. When she had finished, withdrawn the needle and bent Jed's arm up over a pressure pad against the vein, he produced a small cup of liquid, lifted Jed's head and tipped it into his mouth.

He swallowed convulsively, the reflex triggered by the liquid in his throat, and Gabby was relieved to see he was not as deeply unconscious as she had feared. She thought it might be safer, that being the case, to give him medicines orally instead of intravenously in view of the absence of sterile saline solution as a carrier.

The *dukun* was now fishing about in his bag and pulling out a variety of things—brilliantly coloured feathers, a shrivelled frog, some claws off a nameless animal, a piece of fur—there seemed no end to the bizarre collection of items he came up with. He laid them in a ring around Jed's head and began to chant, and Gabby settled back to watch.

Clearly, this was the theatre of his work, the drink having been the real treatment. This spectacle was now for psychosomatic relief, the psychology of medicine that was so effective in witchcraft and African juju.

She knew it wouldn't hurt him, and there was nothing she could do. Who could tell—perhaps the ritual would invoke the help of some god she had never heard of? At this point, she wasn't prepared to turn away any aid at all—cerebral malaria could and did kill in six hours.

She closed her eyes and hugged her arms tight around her body. Please, no, don't let him die, she said silently. Don't take him away from me now when I've only just found him. Don't let me lose him like this.

There was a soft touch on her shoulder, like a butterfly, and she opened her eyes to find the *dukun* regarding her compassionately. He patted her hand and then, beckoning, he went out of the hut.

She followed him down the ladder and across to Hari's hut. Hari! Heavens, in the confusion she'd forgotten all about the young woman!

She was lying propped up on brightly coloured rugs, a baby in each arm, and she looked wide awake and well. When she saw Gabby she smiled broadly and beckoned her over. Gabby knelt down beside her and hugged her, then sat back and looked at the babies.

She wanted to say, 'How are you? The babies are beautiful, you're a lucky girl. I hope you aren't in too much pain.' But it was impossible. Perhaps her face said it for her. Whatever, she couldn't keep the smile off it.

She patted Hari's abdomen and raised her eyebrows in enquiry, and Hari pulled a little face. So she was in pain, but not so bad that she couldn't hold her babies and feed them, with help. Her mother was there, of course, beaming broadly and pressing Gabby's hand to her head in a gesture of gratitude.

Gabby checked the incision and found the dressing had been replaced by a poultice of leaves bruised in hot water, by the look of it, and the incision line under the leaves looked clean and healthy and without any sign of infection.

Yet. She hoped it would continue.

She smiled her satisfaction to Hari, who was obviously nearly as proud of her stitches as she was of her babies. They offered her coffee and more of the little palm cakes, and she was going to refuse before she saw the look in Hari's eyes. The new mother wanted company, and to show off her babies to her new friend who had helped to save their lives, and Gabby didn't have the heart to refuse.

So she sat and drank a quick cup of the thick coffee and ate two of the little cakes. Then, bowing to the *dukun* who was busy mixing something in the corner, she left them and went back to Jed.

'How is he?' she asked Sue anxiously. 'I had to go and see Hari and there didn't seem to be a polite way to get out of it.'

'He's the same. He doesn't seem any worse, anyway,

and he's a bit less fidgety. He's talking, though—something about angels?'

Gabby gave a shaky little laugh, wondering what on earth he'd said. 'Angels?'

His lids fluttered and he looked straight at her, his eyes sparkling a vivid blue. 'My favourite angel,' he slurred. 'The angel Gabrielle herself. I love you. C'm'ere, you sexy thing.'

They fluttered shut again, to Gabby's relief, and he went quiet.

Sue laughed. 'Oh, well, at least we know he's not dreaming about dying. He spooked me for a minute. Want any more help?'

Gabby looked around. The room was hot and stuffy, and she wondered if there was any way to ventilate it better.

'It's getting so hot,' she murmured to herself. 'I wonder if we can cool him down?'

'You might find it cooler under the hut in the shade—shall I get the men to carry him out for you? You probably ought to sponge him down too, he's still very hot.'

'I think so—yes, please, Sue, could you do that?'

She waited until Sue had left the room and then tugged Jed's briefs on more or less properly. He was heavy and uncooperative, though, and it wasn't easy. Sue came back with Ismail and Luther, and they took an end each and carried him, slung between them, out of the hut and down the ladder to the shady spot underneath.

Gabby carried the mats and rugs and made up a bed on the ground, and they laid him down in the cooler air and then sat beside her. Sue fetched cool water and a cloth, and Gabby sponged him down, keeping an eye on the time.

He would need oral therapy, if she could get it into

him, as soon as possible, but for now she wanted to keep sponging and see if she could lower his temperature. It seemed to be climbing even higher, and every now and then he had a rigor, a shuddering fit almost like a convulsion.

People came and went, sitting quietly with her for company and helping her with the endless little tasks. Hari's mother sat for a while, and her sister, and Sue was never far away.

Derek spent some time talking to Jamal about the situation back at base, but he was still quite weak and spent a lot of the day resting. Gabby, though, didn't rest. There wasn't time.

The *dukun* came and gave Jed more of the vile green decoction, and she managed to crush up the malaria pills and dissolve them in honey and coax him to swallow the mixture. That in itself took nearly an hour.

During the afternoon Sue came and sat down with her back against one of the posts and regarded Gabby thoughtfully. 'You look awful. Why don't you let me take over and go and have a sleep? You were up all night with Hari, and you'll have days of this ahead of you. You ought to pace yourself.'

It made sense, but she didn't dare leave him. She went down to the pool, though, and washed herself and her clothes by the simple expedient of walking into the water fully clothed. She washed out Jed's clothes as well, and then went back and changed into the sarong.

Her shoulders were bare, but in view of the near-nakedness of the other women she didn't think it would matter. She smothered herself in insect repellent, hung the clothes over a beam and went back out to Jed.

'Go and lie down for a while,' Sue ordered her.

'I can't. I won't sleep. I need to be with him.'

Sue sat back on her heels and regarded Gabby

thoughtfully. 'You love him very much, don't you?' she said shrewdly.

There was no point in lying. 'Yes,' she replied. 'I do. I can't let him die, I know that.'

She plucked at his skin. It was still plump and taut, but she needed to keep getting fluids into him if she could or he might become dehydrated. 'Help me give him a drink,' she said to Sue, and together they propped him up and dribbled cool boiled water into his mouth.

He swallowed barely any, most of it dribbling out of the corner of his mouth and running down his chest. Sometimes, though, he did swallow, and for those few times it was worth it.

She stayed with him all that day and all the following night, and as dawn broke on the second day the *dukun* came back and squatted down beside her in the hut. He said something she couldn't understand, and then some men came and lifted Jed up like a rag doll and carried him outside under the hut again.

She made as if to follow, but the old man pointed to her bed and ordered her to stay.

'But I need to look after him,' she argued.

However, he was having none of it. There was no need for language. He simply pointed to her, pointed to the bed and walked out, dropping the bark-cloth door curtain into place as he left. He might just as well have locked it, the meaning was so clear.

Exhausted, beyond thought, she lay down obediently and slept for two hours. Then she woke up in a panic and got up and went to Jed, to find a strange woman bathing him with cool water.

The woman smiled at her and patted the ground beside her, and she sat down and looked at him.

He was still alive, despite her desertion. Gabby's shoulders drooped with relief, and she opened the flight

bag and took out the next dose of quinine, pyrimethamine and sulphonamide. She crushed the tablets into the
honey and smeared the paste on his tongue, then stroked
the underneath of his jaw to stimulate the swallowing
reflex.

As she did so she noticed that his skin was beginning
to show signs of dehydration, and he was still almost
unconscious. She propped him up and gave him a drink,
and was rewarded by him dribbling over her trousers.

'Really, Jed, I've just done the washing!' she grumbled, and to her surprise he turned towards her voice and
mumbled something.

'Jed?'

'Head aches,' he said almost inaudibly. She bent and
pressed her lips to his forehead, and he moaned softly
and turned his face into the softness of her breasts.

'Gorgeous,' he mumbled. 'Sexy, sexy lady. I want to
make love to you.'

She looked up to see Derek there, grinning, and went
beetroot red.

'Don't be silly, you're sick,' she reminded him a little
breathlessly.

'Not silly—love you. Marry me, angel.'

She smiled. 'Of course I will—just as soon as you're
better. Now go to sleep.'

'Sick, Gabby,' he mumbled. 'Head hurts.'

'I know,' she murmured soothingly, and smoothed his
hair back from his face, forgetting Derek. Jed was hot
and she tried to move away a little but he hung on, and
so she held him like that for ages while the tears ran
down her face and dripped onto his hair. Eventually she
felt the light touch of the *dunku* on her shoulder.

She lifted her head with a sigh, and he tutted at her
and moved her out of the way. More of the vile green

liquid was coaxed into Jed, and more incantations were said, and Gabby joined in with prayers of her own.

Then he gathered up his trappings and beckoned Gabby to follow him to his hut. There he gave her food and drink, and if there was anything in it she didn't care. She was sure now he was a good man, and any fears Jed might have had about him being a quack had been long dispelled. If he wanted to give her medicine for anything let him, she thought.

Anyway, she was starving.

She ate the rice and vegetables and some of the sauce, drank the coconut milk and stood up. 'I have to go back to Jed,' she told him, not expecting him to understand, but he nodded.

'Jed,' he said, and let her go.

He was hovering on the fringes constantly for the next few days, quietly coming and going, taking care of her and Jed and Hari, and she was immensely grateful for his loyal support.

Derek continued to recover and was much stronger, and the others seemed to be remaining well, to her relief. She had her hands more than full as it was.

Jed, meanwhile, continued to be oblivious of the rest of the world. He kept talking rubbish, some of it utter gibberish, some unfortunately quite easily understandable to the inevitable audience, keeping her company in the shade under the hut.

At one point he opened his eyes and looked at Gabby with a glazed expression. 'You are one hell of a sexy woman,' he told her gruffly. Derek and Luther, sitting nearby, laughed softly, and Gabby felt herself colouring.

'Jed, shut up, you don't know what you're talking about,' she told him.

'Yesido,' he slurred. 'Sexy legs, sexy eyes, sexy everything.'

'You sound drunk.'

'Because I fancy you? C'mere. I wanna hold you—'

'Jed,' she said warningly, and he giggled.

'Never learnt to take a compliment,' he told her, and lunged towards her.

She dodged out of the way and he collapsed on the mats and started to snore. She sighed and glared at him.

'I think I like you better unconscious,' she muttered at his comatose form. 'At least you're less embarrassing.'

He mumbled off and on for the next couple of days, coming and going like a tide as the drugs fought the parasite for supremacy. Then on the morning of the third day he opened his eyes and looked at her.

'I have got one hell of a headache,' he said gruffly. 'Have I been ill?'

To her humiliation she burst into tears, dropping her face into her hands and weeping silently with relief.

'Gabby?' he murmured. 'Gabby, what's the matter?'

She sniffed hard and pulled herself together with an effort. 'You've had malaria.'

'Again?' he said heavily. 'Damn. What sort?'

'Cerebral—falciparum malaria, we think.'

His eyes widened. 'Really? No wonder my head hurts.'

She nodded. 'I've been following the instructions and treating you, and the *dukun* has been giving you something green and gruesome and chanting over you—whatever, it seems to have worked…'

She swallowed the tears again and gave him a rather watery smile. 'It's nice to have you talking sense. You've been a bit—well, away with the fairies.'

He groaned and rolled his eyes. 'Sorry.' He moved his head and groaned again. 'Could I have a drink?' he asked.

'Sure.' She poured some cool, boiled water out of a big container into a coconut shell and held it to his lips, and he sipped it and lay back.

'Thanks,' he sighed, and then his eyes drifted shut and he slept again. He continued like that off and on for the rest of the day, and although there were no more episodes of delirium he was still a bit confused and obviously sick.

That night, though, for the first time he seemed to be sleeping normally and, when she checked it, his skin seemed to be a normal temperature.

Relieved that he seemed to have turned the corner, she relaxed and slept heavily for the first time in almost a week, and when she woke he was gone.

'Jed?' she called, scrambling out of bed and pulling on her clothes.

Sue stuck her head round the doorway. 'Derek's taken him down to the pool for a wash—he felt hot and sticky. He wants to know what drugs he's had so I told him he'd have to ask you. He seems fine.'

Gabby sighed with relief and sagged against the wall. 'I didn't know where he was. I thought he might have wandered in his sleep.'

Sue laughed. 'No, just gone to freshen up. I can hear them coming back now.'

Sue's head disappeared and Gabby gathered up the bedclothes and took them down under the hut in the shade. Jed was sitting against a post, looking exhausted after his exertions, but at least he looked a little fresher.

'Feel better?' she asked him, arranging the bedclothes.

'Much. Thanks—I think I'll have a rest. I feel so weak.'

'I'm not surprised, you've been at death's door,' Derek told him bluntly.

Jed rolled over onto his hands and knees and crawled

onto the bedding, then collapsed. 'Tell me about it,' he muttered.

The others left them so Gabby could settle him to sleep, but after a moment he opened his eyes again. 'I don't suppose there are any headache pills in that flight bag?' he asked her.

'Paracetamol,' she told him.

'I'll have two—and what treatment have you been giving me?'

She helped him take the pills, then sat down beside him with the drug chart she'd improvised on the back of the leaflet and told him what he'd had and when.

'How long have I been out of it?' he asked in puzzlement when she started to list the third day.

'Four days altogether,' she told him.

He looked thoughtful. 'Oh. Right. I can remember odd bits and pieces but I didn't realise it was that long.' He took her hand, but didn't meet her eyes. 'Look, Gabby, I don't know what I said and did—I gather some of it was pretty embarrassing. It's just the way I am with malaria. It makes me a bit unihibited—just ignore it, and if I offended you I'm sorry. I've been known to do all sorts of things in the past but it doesn't mean anything.'

She grinned. 'Forget it, Jed, you didn't do anything.'

'I didn't? Good. Only I wouldn't want to have embarrassed you.' He gave a wry laugh. 'I gather I asked you to marry me once—crazy. I hope you had the good sense to ignore it. It doesn't mean anything.'

Her heart jerked painfully. 'Yes, of course I did,' she said with a little laugh. Was it as hollow as it sounded to her?

He closed his eyes and sank back against the bedclothes. 'I don't suppose there's anything interesting to drink, is there?'

'Drink?' she said numbly. 'Yes, of course. I'll get you something.'

Just ignore it? she thought. It doesn't mean anything? Nothing? None of it? Not the love-making before, either?

Of course, she realised with a shock, he'd had malaria then. Probably Hari's operation was the last thing he'd done when in full control of his faculties. So when he'd told her he loved her was that just the malaria speaking?

Hot colour scorched her cheeks when she thought of the uninhibited way she'd responded. Well, if she was lucky he wouldn't remember any of it, and so she could pretend it hadn't happened and spare them both some embarrassment.

She got some fresh coconut milk in a cup and took it in to him, and he drank it eagerly—too eagerly.

'Steady, not too much at once,' she cautioned, taking it away, and he lay down again and gave her a wry grin.

'So, what's happened while I've been out of it?' he asked after a moment.

'Not much to anyone else. Hari's much better.'

'Hari?' He blinked. 'Did I dream it, or did we—? No, we couldn't have done.'

Do what? she wondered. Make love?

'Tell me we didn't do a Caesarean section by candle-light with only herbal anaesthesia.'

So he didn't remember—yet. 'We did. She's fine, incidentally, so are the babies.'

'Babies?' Jed repeated, half sitting up then falling back with a groan and clutching his head. 'Oh, God, I want to die.'

He rolled to his side and shut his eyes, and seemed to sleep for a while. She left him to sleep until it was time for his drugs again, then she washed his face and hands and changed the rug over him for a cooler, drier one.

'I gather you looked after me almost on your own.' he said quietly as she finished.

She avoided his eyes. 'Yes, most of the time. The *dukun* helped, and so did some of the women—they sponged you down and helped me give you drinks and medicines.'

'I don't remember it. I remember hearing people talking to me and making me drink something ghastly, but nothing else. I just know it seemed endless.' He looked up at her. 'You look bloody awful,' he told her bluntly. 'Have you had any sleep?'

Sexy legs, sexy eyes, sexy everything? Only in his delirium, evidently. 'A bit last night. You kept me rather busy before that,' she told him, perhaps rather sharply because he seemed to withdraw.

'I'm sorry. I'm very grateful. I would have died without your help.'

She choked back the sob of protest. 'You didn't, though. That's all that matters. Get some rest now.'

She scrambled to her feet and all but ran down to the pool, then, heedless of any eyes on her, she stripped and dived into the chilly water. Her heart was breaking. She couldn't pretend or hide it any longer, and the noise of the waterfall that filled the pool would at least muffle her grief.

He didn't remember.

She did, though. She thought of the tenderness of his hands, the light in his eyes, the care he had taken with her. She thought of him telling her it was like coming home, and a sob rose in her throat.

Meaningless, all of it. Just empty words.

'Marry me, angel.'

She cried for what seemed like ages, then the chill of

the water drove her out and she wiped the water off her arms and legs and dressed again. When she looked up the *dukun* was standing watching her with gentle, understanding eyes, and another sob tore its way out of her chest.

'I'm just so tired,' she said. She closed her eyes, and the next thing she felt was his arms around her, cradling her very gently as she wept. Then he wiped her eyes with his gnarled old thumbs, patted her shoulder and led her back to the village.

He sent her in to Hari, who took one look at her and made her lie down on a mat in the corner. She was asleep in seconds, and she must have slept for hours.

When she woke, it was to Sue shaking her shoulder and saying something excitedly.

She opened her eyes and struggled into a sitting position, fighting the pins and needles in her arm. 'What?' she mumbled. 'Is it Jed?'

'He's got an e-mail,' Sue told her. 'It's OK, Gabby—help's on its way. We're going to be rescued!'

CHAPTER NINE

GABBY went back to their hut and found everyone in a state of great excitement.

They were clustered round Jed in his bed under the hut, and he was grinning wearily. 'My secretary just got a rise,' he announced. 'Bless her heart, she checked the e-mail, contacted Bill Freeman's office and mobilised a search party, then replied to me, telling me what was happening.'

'What *is* happening?' Gabby asked, her feelings very mixed. She'd made friends in the village, despite the language barrier—Hari and the *dukun*, and some of the other women—and she had felt herself grow closer to Jed over the twelve days they had been there.

Now, it seemed, it was all going to come to an end—possibly in the next day or so—and she wasn't sure how she would go back to her ordinary life. She would miss them—especially Jed, and she was sure their relationship would be over. He'd as good as told her that.

Derek was explaining that a group including Jon and Bill were setting off from Telok Panjang and making their way on foot from the compound, following the river and using the Magellan GCS to communicate with base and with them.

'Unfortunately, I think our battery might be about to give up the ghost,' Derek said. 'Still, at least they know where we are and can make their way towards us.'

'I need to speak to Johannis,' Jed said from his pile of bedding. 'We need him primed to deal with their arrival, and he needs to be sure exactly what it is we're able to negotiate on.'

'I agree,' Derek put in. 'I'm sure the power station will have to go ahead. The only variable will be the positioning of it, and they need to understand that.'

'Don't get overtired,' Gabby warned them both. 'You've both been ill—you must be careful. You never know, you might have to walk out of here and just at the moment you, Jed, particularly, aren't in a fit state to do it.'

'I'm fine, don't fuss,' he told her, and turned back to Derek.

'OK,' she said under her breath. 'Suit yourself.'

She walked off, leaving the others to their endless confab. So he was quite happy to let her wait on him when it suited him, but as soon as it came to taking advice, oh, no, he was fine!

'Men!' she muttered. She walked out of the village along one of the paths, her feet instinctively leading her towards the grave trees. She needed the peace and tranquillity that she found there, the almost church-like atmosphere of hushed reverence.

She was still feeling bruised inside, angry with herself for thinking that all those tender words were real and not just the product of his illness. So she'd thought that the delirium had made him more honest and uninhibited? Apparently, it just made him lie and flatter—perhaps that was the man he really was after all, a womanising flirt with a laughing eye and a ready compliment.

Damn him.

She walked under the towering grave trees and turned her face up to them. They had a quiet dignity that she needed just now, and she sat down against the trunk of one and rested her head back against it.

They were about to be rescued, and she had no idea

how she was going to cope without him. Would she ever
see him again? She doubted it somehow. All the cama-
raderie they'd built up in the week before his illness
seemed to have gone out of the window, and he was
almost like a stranger now.

She stared at the little squares on the trunk of the tree
facing her, and wondered about the women who'd buried
their babies in there. How had they coped?

How much less significant was her own sorrow.

The crackling of a twig startled her, and she saw the
man who'd been so interested in her on the day of their
capture standing a few feet away, his eyes fixed on her.

In his hand was a *parang*, a sharp jungle knife, hanging loosely by his side, and the light in his eyes was
chilling. He must have been waiting all this time to get
her alone.

She swallowed and tried to stare him out, but he didn't
move, except to coil his fingers more tightly round the
handle and slowly raise the knife above his head.

Fear clawed at her. He was going to throw the knife
at her!

He said something, very softly, and held his other
hand up as if telling her to sit still.

'You have to be joking,' she muttered, but then out
of the corner of her eye she caught a movement, a slow,
weaving movement, repetitive—

There was a *swoosh* beside her ear, and she screamed,
darting away from the tree as something thrashed against
her, and then the man caught her in his arms and stopped
her headlong flight, turning her back to face the tree.

The blade of the *parang* was buried in the bark, blood
staining it, and on the ground at the base of the trunk,
still twitching, lay the body of a snake.

'Oh, Lord,' she whispered. Cold sweat broke out on

the palms of her hands, and she scrubbed them against her legs.

Her 'assailant' grinned, picked up the snake and slung it over his shoulder, then picked up the head off the ground and showed it to her, pulling out the flaps of skin on each side.

A cobra. Great. Marvellous.

She gave him a sickly smile. 'Thank you,' she said fervently, and he laughed cheerfully, obviously pleased that she was impressed.

He hooked the *parang* out of the trunk, wiped the blood off it on the undergrowth and turned away, beckoning her to follow him back to the village.

She needed no second bidding. She was right there with him, almost standing on his heels in her haste to get back to safety.

As she entered the clearing Jed looked up from talking to Johannis and his eyes narrowed. She smiled at the man who'd rescued her, and to her surprise he blushed beneath his dark skin and turned away with an embarrassed giggle.

He's just shy, she thought to herself, not shifty at all, and he's fascinated by me, poor deluded boy.

Suppressing a smile, she crossed over to Jed and he glowered at her.

'If you've quite finished consorting with the natives, we've got things to sort out,' he growled. 'I want to send a reply to this e-mail, and we'll need scouts unobtrusively circulating on the outskirts of the village to leave pointers, just in case they get lost. I want you and Sue to go to the washing pool, and take the track from there downstream towards the town. The rest of you take the other tracks—not all at once. Pace yourselves and take turns.

'Leave pointers if you can, footprints of your shoes in

the track—that sort of thing. Of course if it rains it'll mess things up, but they might come before then and if not we'll have to go out and do it again.'

He looked round at everyone. 'Any questions?'

Luther nodded. 'How long will it be before they come?'

'Any time in the next few hours or days, I would guess. That depends whether or not they can find the track, if they can follow it, how many of them there are and so forth. We'll just have to be patient.'

And that, of course, was the problem. Waiting was going to be hell on nerves already stretched taut. Leaving the others, Sue and Gabby set off for the pool and found children laughing and splashing in the water.

'I'll miss the little ones,' Sue told her. 'They're so sweet and friendly, and there's one in particular who keeps bringing me little stones and things as presents.'

Gabby laughed. 'My nephews and nieces do that on walks, and sometimes I can hardly get home for the weight in my pockets!' She lost her smile then, looking round at the women and children. 'I'll miss them, too, especially Hari. She's been really sweet to me, and her babies are so lovely. I hate leaving her before she's properly healed, just in case anything goes wrong, but I suppose we'll have to.'

'I think the *dukun* will look after her,' Sue said confidently. 'He's a wonderful man, they're very lucky to have him. I think Jed wants to get to know him and learn some of his secrets. I shouldn't be at all surprised if he doesn't come back, once we're all released, just to find out more.'

Gabby leant against a tree and toed the earth idly. 'What about you and Derek? Will you stay and finish off the power station if they can agree a new site?'

Sue shrugged. 'I don't know. I didn't intend to get

pregnant, but these things happen and neither of us are getting any younger. We're both thirty-four now so I suppose it's the right time for us. I don't want Derek out here on his own, but on the other hand I don't know how I'd feel about having a baby out here.'

'I wonder if Jon and Penny will stay?' Gabby mused.

'Who knows? If Penny's here it will be easier, of course, and more fun.' Sue shrugged away from her tree and headed off casually down the path. 'Come on, we've got to make tracks, so to speak.'

They were careful to leave pronounced tracks back towards the village, deliberately treading in muddy bits to leave lasting footprints, but, of course, there was no guarantee that they would survive the rain or even be noticed.

'Do try and keep Derek quiet,' Gabby advised as they returned to the village. 'I know he thinks he's better, but he really ought to be careful. He might be less stable now, and the insulin should have been refrigerated, of course, so it might not be as good as it ought to be.'

Sue sighed. 'I'll try, but he's every bit as stubborn as Jed in his way. I'll do my best, though. What are you going to do about Jed?'

Gabby gave a short laugh. 'I think I've been told my services are no longer required,' she said a little bitterly.

'Oh, dear. I wonder if that's Derek's doing? I think he told him this morning about what he'd been saying when he was delirious, and he was apparently very embarrassed and worried he'd humiliated you.'

Gabby laughed awkwardly. 'I think I'm made of sterner stuff than that.' Anyway, it wasn't humiliation that was her problem, it was losing him.

They rejoined the others, but Jed was deep in conversation with Derek, drawing plans and discussing alternative sites and so on, and so she went to see Hari.

She was up and about now, just doing a little bit here and there, but Gabby was very much afraid she'd do too much too soon and burst her stitches. She tried to explain that to Hari in mime, and ended up having to get Johannis, with Jed's help, so she could explain the importance of being careful for the first few weeks.

The wound was healing nicely, she saw when she examined Hari, and her uterus was going down well. The babies were positively blooming, and it seemed almost impossible that five days before they'd been on the point of death.

Gabby stayed with her for lunch, holding one of the babies while Hari ate, and after they'd finished their meal she went back to the others.

'How is she?' Jed asked without preamble.

'All right, I think. Healing well, babes both fine. You did a good job.'

Was it her imagination or did his skin colour? 'Just don't ask me to do anything like that again,' he said gruffly.

Raised voices behind them made him turn his head, then sigh. 'I think the tension's getting to everyone. Waiting now is going to be the hardest part.'

'Waiting is always the hardest part of anything. Waiting for you to come back to us was pretty hellish.'

He looked down at his hands, fiddling with a twig for a moment. 'Thanks for sticking by me,' he muttered. 'I'm sorry I said all those things.'

'Actually, some of them were quite complimentary,' she said with forced brightness.

He shot her a searching look. 'I doubt if any of them did you justice. I gather I was a bit crude at times.'

She blushed and trailed her fingers through the sand, sifting it. 'Look, just forget it, Jed, OK? I have.'

He looked as if he was about to say something else,

but then he shut his mouth and turned back to the twig, tearing it into tiny little pieces. 'Luther's got a low-grade fever and bloody diarrhoea. I think he's got dysentery. Have we got anything to give him?'

'Nothing much. The rest has all been used up. I'll ask the *dukun*.'

'He'll start charging,' Jed said with a smile, the first one he'd given her all day, and she nearly cried.

'I'll bat my lashes.'

She went over to his hut and greeted him, and he put down the stick he was whittling and unfolded his frail form, following her back to the hut. She showed Luther to him, and after laying his hands on him for a moment he disappeared and came back with a few black seeds.

'Papaya seeds,' Luther said weakly. 'It's an old remedy. It works.'

'He's holding up two hands—is that ten a day? An hour?'

'A day,' Luther said. 'You have to chew them.'

'We've got a couple of sachets of electrolyte solution,' Gabby told Jed. 'Shall I make one of them up for him?'

'Yes—give him as much as he can cope with. Hopefully we'll get out of here soon and he can have proper medical attention.'

The papaya seeds seemed to help, and by the end of the afternoon he was feeling a little better although he still had a fever and diarrhoea. The *dukun* brought him something else, a powder that made him sleep and that she suspected might be related to opium. Whatever, he wasn't going to be here long enough to get addicted and sleep was the best thing for him.

It would have been the best thing for Jed, but he was too busy planning to rest. He slept for an hour, but he looked like death warmed up and wouldn't give in.

The rain had come after lunch, of course, drowning out conversation and washing away all their careful tracks, and because it was the start of the rainy season there was a spectacular thunderstorm so even if he'd wanted to sleep it would have been difficult.

Now it was evening, the sky darkening to a velvet blackness in minutes, and they gathered in their hut by the doorway and looked out at the village, settling down for the night.

'I thought we'd be gone,' Derek said, voicing everyone's thoughts and disappointments. 'I thought for sure they would have been here by now.'

'Maybe the rains have held them up,' Gabby suggested. 'Perhaps they've had landslides—some of the tracks round here are showing signs.'

'Maybe they've got lost.'

'With the technology they've got available to them? They could be put down anywhere on earth and know exactly where they were. They aren't lost,' Jed pointed out. 'I expect they've found the village and are waiting for the morning to make their move. I suggest we all get an early night so we're ready for whatever the morning brings.'

'And most particularly you,' Gabby told him firmly, and chivvied him off to bed.

It took some time to settle everyone down, but finally Gabby crawled into her bed next to Jed and lay there, listening to the jungle. After the threat with the snake earlier, it didn't seem quite the friendly place it had seemed before, and she found she was tense with the waiting and unable to sleep.

Jed, too, seemed to be wakeful. She turned her head and found him looking at her in the dim candle light. 'How's Luther?' he asked.

'Still suffering, although less so, and the powder

seemed to help. I'll have to get some more for him in the morning.'

'What about Derek?' he asked in a low undertone.

'I'm concerned about him. I think he's becoming a little hyperglycaemic. Perhaps the insulin's deteriorated with the heat.'

Jed nodded. 'That's what I was afraid of. Please, God, let them come tomorrow.'

She turned on her side, facing him. 'What do you think's holding them up?'

'Not knowing the route? There are lots of ravines and things—if you didn't know the way it could be quite tricky. It wasn't easy even on the right track.'

She chewed her lip for a second. 'What if they can't get to us? What if they never make it?'

'They'll make it,' he promised and, reaching out a hand, he cupped her cheek. His thumb idly stroked her temple, soothing her, and she felt silly tears well in her eyes. She closed them so he wouldn't see, but he must have sensed them because the next minute she was in his arms and he was cradling her against his chest.

'It's all right, Gabby,' he murmured. 'We'll be OK. You'll be out of here soon, you wait and see. It's nearly over, sweetheart.'

She slid an arm around him and moved closer, drawing comfort from his nearness. He was thinner, she realised with a shock. The malaria had drained his resources, and yet here he was, being strong for all of them when they should have been looking after him.

She felt him relax against her, and his breathing become more even. Then, when he was asleep, she let the silent tears slip down her cheeks and soak into his shirt. Was this the last time she'd ever hold him?

'If they don't come today I'm walking out of here.'

'Derek, don't be ridiculous,' Sue told him firmly.

'You'll do no such thing. Without any insulin you wouldn't get anywhere.'

'Well, I can't stay here without it, can I?' he snapped. 'I might as well take my chances in the jungle.'

'You're being absurd. Just rest and conserve your energy, and don't have too much sugary fruit.'

'I'll eat what I bloody well like—'

'Hey, hey, boys and girls, let's not fight. None of us wants to be here under these conditions, and it's almost over. Just bide your time.'

'I'm sure if we got Johannis and Jamal out of their hut we could make it back down—'

'Before they get us with their blowpipes? I don't think so,' Jed said drily. 'They might be friendly and pleasant at the moment because there's nothing at stake, but once they decide if they're going to go and negotiate this change of site we might find we're much more closely guarded. I think at the moment they're keeping us here to make Bill and the government sweat. It suits them to do so, and they know we won't do anything silly without Jamal or Johannis to guide us. That's why they're always so closely guarded.'

'They could have told us the way,' Derek argued. 'We haven't even asked them!'

'You can get lost in the middle of London with an A to Z!' Sue told him bluntly. 'What are they going to say—turn left at the big fern? Get real!'

'Well, we could try—'

'And die in the attempt. Thanks, but no thanks—'

'Hush! What's that?' Gabby said.

They all stopped talking then, cocking their heads and listening.

'Have I gone off my trolley or is that a helicopter?' Jed murmured quietly.

'My God!' Derek said. 'I'll stick my head out of the door and have a squint.'

He left the room, and they waited, listening, until it was obvious that, yes, it was a helicopter and, yes, it was coming in to land, or at least to hover just overhead.

They all ran to the door, to find Derek on the ground, waving frantically at a craft about fifty feet above the ground. The dust was swirling up around the huts, and the villagers were running, screaming, men, women and children scattering in all directions as a hatch opened and a ladder was thrown out.

Bill was the first to descend, followed by Jon, another man in shorts and T-shirt and a government official in a safari suit. As soon as the last one was off the ladder the helicopter lifted up and away, and as the dust settled so the villagers began to creep back out from their hiding places, spears and blowpipes at the ready.

Derek, Sue and the Indonesians ran towards them, but Jed hung back. 'Why couldn't they just walk in?' he muttered, and Gabby turned and looked at him.

'You look like death—you should be lying down.'

'And miss this? No way,' he replied, and then ruined it all by swaying against the ladder and nearly falling over.

'Stubborn fool,' she said firmly and, tucking herself into his armpit, she draped his arm over her shoulder, hung onto his wrist and almost carried him across the clearing to the others.

Then there was lots of hugging and backslapping before Jed called them all to order.

'I think, gentlemen, we should get down to business,' he said. 'Jamal and Johannis are here and ready to translate—I think it might be politically correct to introduce you to the key players. You do understand about the grave trees?'

'Oh, yes,' Bill assured him. 'We've examined the site and agree with you. We can't possibly build it there. We just have to negotiate an alternative.'

Gabby felt the tension drain out of her shoulders. She was sure it would now be all right.

With Gabby supporting him, Jed went over to the edge of the group of villagers, where the chief and the *dukun* were standing together in hastily donned ceremonial garb, and smiled and bowed at them.

'Jamal? Johannis?' Jed asked, and the chief waved at a man who brought the men to the edge of the circle.

'Jamal, ask Johannis to tell them these men have come to talk about the grave trees and to apologise for having threatened the sacred place.'

They waited while the translations were carried out, and then the chief and the *dukun* looked at Jon, Bill and the two other men and bowed their heads slightly.

'The chief says the trees must stay,' Jamal informed her.

'We understand that. There are other ways. Please will they talk about them?'

The message came back that, yes, they would talk.

Jed introduced the chief and the *dukun*, and Jon introduced himself, Bill and the other two, one of whom was from the government, the other from the International Red Cross. The men disappeared under the chief's hut, and Gabby, heart in mouth, followed them and sat down at a polite distance in case she was needed. The others joined her, straining their ears to listen to the conversation.

Coffee was served first, and once the ceremony had taken place the negotiating could begin. She saw the *dukun* produce her drawing, and the government inspector nodded and looked at Bill, who produced a sheaf of paper from his pocket.

The papers were handed backwards and forwards, considered and studied, thought about and argued over, and then once again the *dukun* took them and tucked them into his belt and turned away.

'OK, guys, I think your audience is over,' Jed told them softly. 'Come and see the others. The *dukun* will talk to the elders and consider it. It's all down to him now.'

Jon had brought insulin in case Derek had run out, and Jed tested him and found his blood sugar soaring again. Tutting, he gave him a double dose of the new, fresh insulin, and after an hour he began to feel better again.

Luther, though, was still causing concern and Gabby could tell Jed was worried. What they needed—what they all needed—was to get out of there and have a proper medical check-up. She met Jed's eyes and he winked reassuringly, as if to say, 'Don't worry, it's nearly over.'

Nothing in Indonesia moves fast. It took five hours for the elders to agree—five hours in which the tension rose to unbearable levels. They were closely guarded now, herded together into the hut with Jamal and Johannis, and by the time they were summoned tempers were well and truly frayed.

The key players disappeared again with Johannis and Jamal, and after another hour Jon came up the ladder, grinning.

'You're free to go. We're going to renegotiate the site—we're meeting the elders down there in a couple of days, and we're going to get you all airlifted out of here in the next couple of hours. Gabby, tell me, who's first?'

'Derek,' she said emphatically. 'He needs stabilising in hospital. Sue—she's pregnant and needs checking up.

Luther has dysentery, and Jed's been extremely ill with cerebral malaria and needs proper treatment. The rest of us are well.'

He nodded. 'I'll get those four sent out first, then, and next you and the others, and Bill and I can go last with the interpreter.'

He left the hut and went out to the others, and a very short time later they heard the whop-whop-whop of the returning helicopter.

It returned for Gabby after an hour, and she bid a tearful goodbye to Hari and the *dukun*. As they rose up in the air the village seemed to disappear, swallowed by the trees, vanishing like a myth.

'I'm sure it can't be anything serious.'

'You look awful—you're suffering from lassitude, nausea, tiredness, lack of appetite—you're coming in for a whole battery of tests, young lady, and that's all there is to it. You could have picked up anything.'

She looked at Jed, fit and well now, sitting on the edge of his desk in the tropical diseases hospital she gathered he worked in when he wasn't swanning about in the tropics, and sighed. 'All right, if you insist.'

'We'll keep you in overnight,' he told her, and her silly heart did a crazy leap. She'd see him! That was worth any amount of tests.

'What are you looking for?' she asked him.

'Anything unusual. My secretary will arrange your admission. I have to fly, I've got another clinic, but I'll see you later.'

He patted her shoulder on the way past, leaving her with a sense of emptiness when he had gone. Funny how it seemed so much colder without his presence.

'Miss Andrews?'

She stood up. 'Yes. I gather I have to come in.'

She'd met his secretary, the woman who had had the initiative to check his e-mails, and she now discovered she was extremely efficient. She flipped open a diary, ran her finger down the days and turned to her. 'Tuesday to Wednesday—all right?'

'That's tomorrow.'

'Yes. Is that too short notice? I think he wants to get the results quickly.'

She shook her head. 'That'll do. I've got my things with me, I was going to stay with a friend.'

'In which case, could you make it today? He thought you probably couldn't, but I think he'd prefer it if you were able to.'

'Fine. If I could just use the phone to ring my parents and my friend, I can stay now.'

'Good. Here, use Jed's phone. I'll come and get you in a minute—I'll just notify the ward.'

His office was functional but very pleasant. She wondered what kind of research assistant he was, and how he came to have his own secretary. Perhaps his research into malaria was a little more organised and well orchestrated than she'd realised...

The tests were apparently endless, involving copious blood-letting and samples from every conceivable part of her. They were sent off to labs, and her heart and brain waves were all charted and inspected and reported as normal.

On the Tuesday her parents arrived to visit her and wait with her for the results, and although some might not be available for a few more days they were going to take her home.

Jed didn't seem to be around much during all of this, to her disappointment. She'd missed him so badly in the past two weeks she couldn't imagine how she would get through the rest of her life, but she'd thought at least she'd see him while she was in the same hospital.

He'd popped in the evening before and told her that they'd agreed a new site for the power station and it was now going ahead with everyone's blessing. 'Johannis has apparently been forgiven for his indiscretion because of his part in the negotiations, and he's been allowed back into the tribe, so I'm going back there in a few days to try and find out what I can from the *dukun*. Anyway, someone has to take out Hari's stitches.'

'They will have dissolved by now.'

He grinned. 'Maybe. I ought to check, though.'

'You're a sucker for punishment,' she said with a smile. 'I knew you'd go back. Give Hari my love when you see her.'

'I will. You get some rest now, you're looking peaky.'

And he'd left her alone to consider the fact that he was leaving the country shortly for heaven knew how long. It was silly to feel so bereft. He'd never promised her anything, except, of course, in the throes of malaria, and she could hardly hold him to those extravagant words.

She'd slept fitfully in the strange bed, and now she was up and dressed, sitting on the edge of the bed talking to her parents about the tests and waiting. Would she see him today?

The Nigerian doctor who'd been dealing with her came in and smiled at her and her parents. 'Well, we've got all the results back that we need,' he told them cheerfully. 'There's nothing to worry about, you'll be pleased to know—'

The door opened and Jed came in, wearing a white coat and looking for the first time like a real doctor.

'Ah, Professor,' Dr Mgabe said.

Professor?

Jed? A professor?

'I was just telling your patient that we have all the results now and there's nothing wrong with her at all. In fact, she's a very fit and healthy woman. She is simply pregnant.'

'What?' Gabby took a deep, steadying breath and looked at Jed, hope flaring in her heart. 'What?' she said again.

'You're having a baby, my dear—nothing more complicated than that.'

Jed looked stunned. He stared at her as if he'd seen a ghost, and then with what looked like a huge effort he sucked in a breath and let it out again. 'Well—that's good, I suppose. Nothing nasty. Fine. Right. Well, ah— I suppose this is it. Um—take care. I'll send you a post-card.'

And he turned on his heel and walked out.

'Well, that's it, you can go home just as soon as you're ready,' Dr Mgabe told her with a smile, and he followed Jed out.

'Darling?' Mrs Andrews said softly.

Gabby stood up on wooden legs. 'We'd better go, then. Um—I've got a case—'

'I'll pack it,' her father said quietly. 'Meg, I think she needs a hug.'

'No!' She moved away, holding herself rigid with enormous effort. 'No. Don't touch me. I'm all right. Just get me out of here.'

They did. They put her in the car and drove her home to their farm in Gloucestershire, and her mother made her a drink and put her to bed, and then went out, clicking the door softly shut behind her.

Then and only then did she allow herself to cry…

CHAPTER TEN

JED pulled up at the end of the drive and sat for a moment, looking at the house. Big, built of stone, it looked a real family home—the sort of place you could retreat to, where your family would close ranks around you.

He switched off the ignition and picked up his mobile phone, keying in her number. A woman answered, sounding like her and yet not.

Her mother?

'Mrs Andrews?' he hazarded a guess.

'Yes.'

'Could I speak to Gabrielle, please? It's Jed Daniels.'

There was silence for a second, and then her mother said, 'She's not here.'

'Oh.' Disappointment and relief fought inside him, and disappointment won. 'Can you tell me when she'll be back?'

'Well, she is here and she's not. She's in one of the cottages, but she's not on the phone yet. Can I get her to call you? I'll see her later.'

'Um…' He hesitated, then said, 'I'm at the end of the drive. Perhaps I could just call and see her.'

There was another pause. 'Well, I suppose so—come up to the house. I'll give you directions.'

He pulled up outside the front of the house and Mrs Andrews came down the steps to meet him, wiping her hands on an apron. She'd been baking, he imagined from the smudge of flour on her nose. It made her look more approachable.

She stopped at the bottom of the steps and he got out

of the car. They stood there for a moment, weighing each other up.

'The cottage is over there,' she said without preamble, pointing across a field. 'You have to go back down the drive and take the track off it. She's probably in the garden—go round the back.'

'Are you sure she won't mind?' he asked, suddenly doubtful about the wisdom of this.

'No, I'm not sure of anything except I think it's about high time you came to see her. She's had a lot to cope with, and she could have done with some support.'

He ducked his head. 'I'm sorry. I've been away again—back to Pulau Panjang. It's not very easy to pop in from there.'

'Well, you're here now, that's all that matters. Just don't upset her.'

He scuffed the ground, feeling like a teenager. 'Is she OK? The baby?'

'They're fine. She'll tell you.'

He nodded and got back into the car, turned it around and headed down the drive. She was still standing there on the steps, watching him.

He found the grassy track, followed it and pulled up outside a pretty little cottage, with flowers blooming in colourful disarray all around the front. He cut the engine and got out, closing the door softly.

Crazy. His palms were sweating, his legs felt like jelly and his mouth was dry. For two pins he'd have got back in the car and driven away, but that wouldn't help at all. He retrieved the parcel from the back seat and knocked on the front door, but there was no reply. Taking Gabby's mother's advice, he went round the back to the garden.

She was there, standing with her back to him bending over a rose, and he stood there riveted to the spot and just drank in the sight of her. She was wearing the sarong Jamal's daughter had given her, and it looked soft and faded and well loved.

He thought she was probably naked under it, and desire raked through him just as she straightened and turned, and he realised with a shock that she was still pregnant.

Pain stabbed him, taking his breath, and then common sense resurrected itself and he dragged in a lungful of sultry summer air.

'Hello, Gabrielle,' he said softly, and she looked up and froze.

'Jed,' she whispered, the roses she had just picked falling unheeded at her feet.

He bent and picked them up, handing them back to her with trembling fingers. 'How are you?' he asked gruffly, and cleared his throat. God, how could he behave normally when all he wanted to do was drag her into his arms and tell her how much he'd missed her?

'All right. What brings you here? Run out of research material?'

She turned and went back towards the cottage and he followed her into the kitchen. 'I've finished. I've brought some photos to show you—of Hari and the babies, and all the others.'

'How are they?' she asked with a smile.

'Fine. Gorgeous. You're a legend over there, you know—the woman that bullied the *dukun*.'

She laughed. 'Someone had to force the issue. She was dying.'

'Yes.' He put down the bag he'd brought from the car and propped his hips against the worktop, looking at her. She'd filled the kettle and was getting mugs down out of a cupboard.

'Tea?' she asked.

'Anything.' He looked at her swollen body and felt a great surge of protective instinct. 'I thought you would have had the baby by now,' he said, struggling for small talk.

'No—it's not due for another fortnight.'

'Oh.' Funny, he'd thought— Oh, well, never mind. He hadn't been thinking clearly then. 'You—um—you haven't got married?'

'Married?' She dropped two teabags into a pot and looked at him. 'No, I haven't got married. Should I have done?'

'I thought—maybe the father—?'

Something happened in her eyes, something sad that made him want to take her in his arms. Anger flickered inside him at the unknown man.

'The father isn't interested,' she told him bluntly.

'Oh.' How could he not be? How could any man turn away from her and her child? Hell, he couldn't, and it was nothing to do with him!

'Is there—um—you know—any—ah—other man—?'

She eyed him straight. 'No, Jed, there's no other man.' She turned to pour the water on the teabags. 'No one at all.'

Hope dawned in him, but he suppressed it. She wasn't interested. She'd said so, at the top of her voice on Monkey Skull Island.

His next words came unbidden, without permission.

'I've missed you.'

She looked up at him sharply and looked away. 'Have you?'

'Yes. Every day.' He looked down at his fingers. 'Funny, I never knew you were missing from my life until I met you, and since then nothing's felt the same.' He gave a short laugh. 'Crazy, isn't it?'

'Jed, what are you trying to say?'

He looked up at her but he couldn't read her expression. She was good at hiding her feelings—all those years of nursing, he supposed.

'I don't know. Only that I want you in my life, and—well, I know it's different these days and loads of women have babies on their own, but if you didn't want to—well, I'm around—'

'Are you offering to be there for the birth?' she asked somewhat incredulously.

'Well—not exactly. Yes, if you wanted me to, but I had in mind perhaps the next fifty-odd years, really.' He swallowed. Hell, this was difficult. He'd never proposed to anyone in his life and he was floundering like a beached whale. 'I think I'm asking you to marry me.'

She gave him a suspicious look. 'Have you got malaria?'

He laughed, a little nervously. 'No, of course not.'

'I just wondered. So, why would you want to marry me?'

He stared at her. 'Because I love you.' He waved a hand. 'I know you don't necessarily love me, but I promise I'd look after you and the baby, and treat it as if it were my own, and perhaps later we could have others, if you wanted…' He trailed to a halt and stopped.

'Forget it. I can see it doesn't appeal. I'm sorry.'

'Oh, you're wrong,' she said softly. 'It does appeal—it appeals enormously. I just wondered what changed your mind about me.'

His brows pleated together. 'Changed my mind? When?'

'When we came home. Well, before, really, but you were very preoccupied and you'd been ill so I could forgive that, but when that doctor told us all I was pregnant you just said goodbye and went, in seconds. I thought you hated me.'

'Hated you? I loved you. I was going to get you better and finish my research, and when everything had settled down again I was going to ask you out, but then I realised that there must be someone else and I felt a fool. You'd told me, after all, that there wasn't anyone so it came as a bit of a surprise.'

'There wasn't.'

'So when—if the baby's not due yet,' he said, going back to the thing that was nagging in his mind, 'when did you—? Was it after we came back?'

She shook her head.

'So there had been someone.'

'No. It happened in Indonesia. I met someone and fell in love.'

Pain stabbed him again. 'Oh. I see.' He cast his mind back through the time they'd been together, and drew a blank. 'Who?' he asked. 'Not your cousin, surely, or Derek?'

'No.'

'Bill.' He said it flatly, as if it left a bad taste in his mouth.

'No. Not Bill.'

'One of the Indonesians, then? Luther?'

She shook her head. 'You've forgotten someone, Jed.'

He thought of the young man who'd lusted after her. He'd seen them coming out of the jungle, laughing, the day before they'd been released. Had they started a relationship while he'd had malaria?

'Who?' he asked hoarsely.

'You.'

The word didn't register for a moment, and when it did he felt the blood drain from his face. 'Me?' he said soundlessly.

His eyes dropped to the swollen abdomen under the sarong, and a great lump formed in his throat. 'Me?' he

said again, and emotion rose up and choked him. He
turned his head, fighting the foolish tears that prickled
at the back of his eyes.

'But—I'd remember—'

'You had malaria.'

He looked back at her, seeing the truth in her eyes,
and the tears spilt over and splashed onto his shirt. 'Why
didn't you tell me—'

He scrubbed a hand through his hair and fought for
composure. 'Damn it, all this time you've needed me
here to look after you and you didn't tell me—Gabby, I
missed you so much—'

His voice cracked and he scooped her into his arms,
hugging her fiercely to his chest. He could hardly reach
her for the baby between them so he hooked out a chair
with his foot and sat down, pulling her onto his lap and
burying his face in her soft breasts.

Wave after wave of emotion washed him—relief,
shock, love, hope for the future—swamping him so that
he could hardly think.

'I ought to be able to remember,' he said eventually.
'Imagine doing something so fundamental as making a
baby and not remembering it afterwards.'

'You were very ill. It was right at the beginning—
straight after we operated on Hari. We stayed up till
dawn, then went to bed and—well, it just happened.'

He tipped his head back and looked into her eyes,
striving for a memory. 'Was it all right? I didn't hurt
you or anything? If I was delirious I might not have been
very communicative—'

'You were wonderful,' she said softly and, bending
her head, she kissed him, then slipped off his lap and
took his hand. 'Come to bed,' she murmured.

'But—the baby—'

'The baby's fine. I'm not. I've missed you so much.'

Her façade crumbled and tears welled in her eyes. 'I thought you didn't love me. I thought you just wanted me out of your life. I thought you thought the baby was just the excuse you needed—'

'Sounds like you thought much too much,' he said gently.

'I've had nothing else to do for eight months.'

'Oh, darling.' He wrapped an arm round her shoulders and squeezed. 'Where's the bedroom?'

'Here.' She pushed open a door and they went into a pretty, airy little room with white bedlinen and soft, floaty curtains.

It made him smile, but only until they reached the bed. Then she freed the top of the sarong and it fell to her feet, and his breath jammed in his throat.

Reaching out trembling hands, he laid them on the warm skin of her abdomen, over his child, and tears welled in his eyes again. 'Oh, angel,' he murmured brokenly. 'I love you so much.'

She undid his shirt buttons and pushed the garment off his shoulders, then freed his belt. His fingers came back to life and he stripped off the rest of his things and lifted her, setting her down gently in the middle of the bed.

'Are you sure this is all right?' he asked.

'It's fine. It might be a little complicated, but it's possible, I'm told.'

He laughed softly, then sobered. 'Just stop me if I hurt you or it's uncomfortable.'

She didn't stop him. She just held him, and cried out, and he lost himself in the magic of her body. She was right, it was complicated, but it was beautiful to hold her, to feel the child kick against his abdomen and know that it was his.

It reduced him to tears again but it didn't matter because Gabby was crying too, and he just shifted so he was lying on his back and she was on her side, one leg draped over him, and he held her tight until their hearts slowed and their tears dried on their cheeks.

'OK?' he asked her, and she nodded, her hair like a halo around her head. He stroked it, loving the feel of it—the feel of her.

'I feel as if I've come home,' he said softly, and she lifted her head and stared at him.

'You said that before.'

'Did I? I've never felt like this with anyone else. It just seems so right to be here with you like this.'

'Good. It needs to because it's where you're going to be for a jolly long time, Professor Daniels.'

He felt his skin colour. 'Don't call me that, I hate it.'

She laughed softly at him. 'I thought they were joking at first. I didn't realise you were a real professor. It was only then that I realised your research might actually be valid and genuine, you know.'

'I kept telling you.'

'I know. I just didn't listen. I'm sorry.'

He hugged her. 'Don't be. It's all right—now.' He shifted his head so he could see her. 'Perhaps you'd want to tell your mother you're OK. She was a bit wary about me.'

'Of course she was. She knows you're the father of her grandchild, and she thinks you dumped me.'

'I had malaria! Anyway, you didn't seem to want to know. I didn't want to push myself in where I wasn't welcome.'

'I'll speak to her. I suppose she'll want to start planning a wedding. It'll have to be September or October now, of course—'

'What?' He sat bolt upright and looked down at her. 'Sorry, darling. I'm an old-fashioned man. This baby's

going to be born in wedlock if it kills me—just resign
yourself to getting married in about three days. If you
want a big palaver with lots of relatives, we can have a
church wedding later with all the pomp and circum-
stance you could dream of, but we're getting married
just as soon as the registrar can do the paperwork.'

To his relief she smiled. 'Good. I agree. I just didn't
want to hassle you. I don't want a big wedding at all,
just a few friends and family.'

Women had a gift for hyperbole, Jed discovered three
days later. 'A few friends and family' turned out to be
over fifty people, a hastily erected marquee and a catered
finger buffet.

'Thank God you didn't want a big wedding,' he said
laughingly to her as they stood side by side, preparing
to cut the cake.

'What?' She looked round and chuckled. 'This is
Mum. I had nothing to do with it. I was busy trying to
find a dress that didn't look like another marquee or a
set of net curtains in a stiff breeze.'

He hugged her, laughing till the tears ran down his
face, and then held her at arm's length. 'You look beautiful,' he assured her proudly. 'I can't wait to get you
away from here.'

'Where are we going?' she asked for the hundredth
time, but he just smiled and refused to tell her. 'You'll
find out,' he promised. 'Now, smile for the birdie, the
cameraman wants our attention again.'

'Open your eyes.'

She looked around at the elegant façade of the familiar
and very exclusive hotel and smiled. 'It's lovely. It's
always been one of my dreams to come here. How on

earth did you find a hotel like this so close to home with a vacancy at this time of year?'

He grinned, obviously pleased with himself. 'Easy. Friends run it. They were able to jiggle it, but only for three days.' He slid out from behind the wheel and came round to open her door. 'We've got a little private lodge on the edge of the woods, with its own hot tub and maid service and telephone, and we can either have room service or eat in the main building, depending on what you want.'

'Room service,' she said instantly, making him laugh. She grinned. 'I do. I don't want to get up at all the whole time we're here. I can't think of anything more wonderful than lying about in a hot tub and relaxing. They can send the food over and you can feed me.'

'You'll come out like a prune.'

'I don't care. I just want to be pampered.'

His eyes darkened. 'Good, because I have lots of that in mind for you.'

'I said pampered, not seduced.'

He laughed again and helped her out of the car, then, offering her his arm, he led her inside. It was cool, the interior lofty and quietly elegant. It must be costing a fortune, she thought, and then put it out of her mind. It was once in their lives, and she was going to love every second of it.

'Mr and Mrs Daniels,' he said to the girl behind the reception desk.

'Ah, yes. You've got the honeymoon lodge. I'll get Nick to take you over.'

A young man in livery appeared and showed them down a tree-lined path to the little lodge, nestling in the trees at the edge of the park. 'I'll bring your car round with your luggage, sir,' he said to Jed, and disappeared, leaving them to look round.

Gabby sat on the comfy sofa and bounced. 'Oh, it's lovely—soft but firm. I wonder what the bed's like?'

He opened a door and whistled, and she got up and went and peered round him. 'Oh, my. A four-poster.'

'And French doors out to the private patio with hot tub.'

'Mmm.'

'Just hang on. He'll be back in a minute with the car and you can do what you like.'

Jed's BMW slid to a halt outside, and Nick came in with the keys and the cases. 'There's champagne on ice on the house, and the hot tub's full and ready to go. Will there be anything else, sir?' he asked.

'No, thank you, that's fine.' He handed him a folded note, took the keys and turned to Gabby. 'Right, my darling, about this tub.'

They played in it for ages, sipping champagne, then moved to the bed and made love slowly and languorously. Room service brought a light supper of cold smoked salmon and salad with fresh crusty rolls, and they curled up on the sofa and watched a soppy old film on the television, before going to bed early.

The next day was more of the same, and by the evening she was feeling totally relaxed.

The next day, though, she woke with dull backache. 'I thought the bed was a bit soft,' she said ruefully. 'That's the price you pay for comfort.'

'Turn over,' Jed ordered gently, and rubbed her back, then nibbled her neck.

She laughed and swatted him away. 'I'll have breakfast in the hot tub,' she told him, and slid her feet over the side of the bed and vanished into the bathroom. By the time she came out he'd uncovered the tub, called room service and their coffee and croissants were on the way.

He fed her in the tub, little bites of croissant with rich strawberry conserve, and trailed little nibbly kisses over her neck and throat as she swallowed.

She giggled and swatted him away again. 'Stop it, you're tickling me.'

'Sorry.' He put down the plate, took her into his arms and kissed her thoroughly. 'Is that better?'

Would she never tire of looking into those beautiful blue eyes?

'Much better,' she said with a smile.

His hand ran lightly over her abdomen and left a shivery trail in its wake. 'How can I be so pregnant and you still want me?' she asked, faintly amazed. 'Come to that, how can I still want you?'

His mouth quirked in a smile. 'We always did have something pretty explosive in the way of chemistry,' he reminded her. 'Hopefully, Mrs Daniels, we always will.'

She ran her finger over his jaw, feeling the stubble and remembering Pulau Panjang. 'Mmm, we did. Call me Mrs Daniels again, I like the sound of it.'

'Mrs Daniels. Mrs John Daniels.'

She swivelled her head. 'Why *are* you Jed and not John?'

'Because my father's John, and the alternative was Jack. I didn't fancy being called after a whiskey so I opted for my initials—John Edward Daniels. Simple.'

'It doesn't sound like a professor.'

He grimaced. 'I hate being a professor. It sounds so erudite and formal.'

'Or mad. I shall have to watch you as you grow older. Only five years to go and you're forty. Maybe you'll go off the rails then.'

'I thought, according to you, I already was.'

'Ah, but you had the good taste to marry me.'

He grinned. 'So I did.' He bent his head and blew the

bubbles away from the slope of her breasts, then trailed a finger across the pale skin. 'I don't suppose you want to finish this off in bed?' he asked softly.

She smiled and held out her hand, and he stood up and pulled her to her feet. As he did so she felt a massive tightening in her abdomen, a hugely powerful gathering of forces. Her eyes widened. 'Jed?'

'What is it?'

'I think we're going to have to put off finishing this for a while,' she said, struggling to breathe normally.

'What's wrong?'

The cramp eased and she smiled uncertainly at him. 'I think I'm in labour.'

His jaw dropped, and then he scooped her up and carried her through to the bedroom, setting her down gently on the bed. 'I'll call for a doctor.'

She laughed. 'You are a doctor. Just give me a minute and I'll get dressed and we can go to the hospital. It's only a few minutes away.'

He sat down, and a moment later she had another contraction, this one even more powerful. She tried to relax, but it was just too strong and she had to push—

'Aagh!'

Jed ran for the phone and called Reception, and told them to get a doctor to them quickly. Then he ran back.

'Just stay with me,' she panted. 'You can deliver it— you delivered Hari's by Caesarean section in candlelight with a kitchen knife and they all survived—I'm sure we'll be all right.'

He took her hands and held them tight. 'I love you,' he told her fervently. 'Just remember that when you end up hating me because I got you pregnant.'

She laughed. 'I won't hate you. I love you much too much—oh!'

Ten minutes later, when the door opened to admit the

doctor and the receptionist, Jed was sitting on the side of the bed with his daughter in his arms and a rather thunderstruck smile on his face.

'Good job I hurried,' the doctor said drily.

Gabby just smiled. She was glad the doctor had been too late because nothing on earth could compare with being alone with Jed and seeing his face when he lifted their baby in his hands...

EPILOGUE

HE LOOKED like something out of an old B-movie.

Faded khaki shirt and shorts, feet propped up on the veranda, hat tipped over his face, chair tilted onto its back legs—and he was in the shade. Gabby should have disliked him on sight.

His shirtsleeves were rolled up to expose deeply tanned and hair-strewn forearms, rippling with lean muscle, and long, rangy legs strewn with more of the same gold-tinged wiry hair stuck out of the bottoms of crumpled shorts. His feet were bare and bony, with strong, high arches and little tufts of hair on the toes. They were at her eye level as she approached the steps to the veranda, and a little imp inside her nearly tickled them.

She couldn't see his face because of the battered Panama hat tipped over his eyes, but his fingers were curled loosely around a long, tall glass of something that looked suspiciously like gin and tonic. The side of the glass was beaded with tiny droplets of water, and in the unrelenting tropical heat it drew her eyes like a magnet.

She reached for the glass.

'Don't even think about it.'

She blinked at the deep growl that emerged from under the hat. She thought she saw the gleam of an eye, but she wasn't sure. He hadn't moved so much as a single well-honed muscle.

'I'm thirsty.'

'So get your own. I need this, I've been busy.'

She poked her tongue out and his arm snaked out and grabbed her leg, hooking her closer. His hand slid up the inside of her thigh and curled possessively around it, his palm icy from the glass. 'Go and put on something with long sleeves, and some sensible shoes and trousers. I've got a surprise for you.'

Long sleeves? She'd been about to head for one of the resort's many pools. 'What about Bethany?'

'She's all ready. We're waiting for you.'

'You've got shorts on.'

'I'll change.'

The chair crashed to the floor and he unfolded himself, tipped back his hat and grinned at her, clearly pleased with himself.

'Where are we going?'

He tapped the side of his nose. 'Just go and change.'

She did, wondering what on earth he had in mind. A trip to Monkey Skull Island? Hardly a surprise—they'd done it once. The power-station site? Ditto.

It was too far to the village, the only other place she really wanted to go, and not even Jed was mad enough to have hired a helicopter.

He scooped Bethany out of her playpen and blew raspberries on her tummy while Gabby changed, then fastened her securely into the baby seat of Sue's and Derek's Jeep that mysteriously seemed to appear just around the corner in the shade.

They headed up the hill out of the resort, past Telok Panjang and the bungalows where Jon and Penny and their children and Sue and Derek and their little boy lived, and up towards the power station. The road was vastly improved—but she knew that, just as she knew that the grave trees and their surroundings were now protected by an enclosure, with a sign that explained what they were and asked people to treat the area with respect.

'This,' she said drily, 'is not a surprise. We've been here.'

He just smiled and turned into a clearing in front of the resited power station, and there, sitting on the ground, was a gleaming white helicopter with *Freeman* written on the side in red.

She looked at Jed. 'Where *are* we going?' she asked, excitement catching her for the first time. 'Tell me, dammit. We're going to the village, aren't we?'

He just grinned, lifted the baby out of her seat in the back and straightened her sun hat, then headed towards the helicopter.

'Hi, Bill. All ready?'

The developer grinned down at Gabby from the cockpit. 'Morning, Gabby. Happy anniversary.'

She climbed up beside him. 'Morning. Thank you. Jed, where are we going? Is it the village?'

But Bill fired up the engine and the rotors started to turn, drowning out his reply. The door slammed, they were strapped in and then they were off, swooping low over the canopy and following the line of the river up into the hills.

Suddenly a tiny clearing appeared ahead, not much more than a gap in the trees, and Bill was setting them down on the familiar patch of bare earth in the centre of the village.

He cut the engine and opened the door so that they could climb out, and as they stepped out into the sunshine the wide-eyed children started to seep back out of the fringe of trees.

'Gabby?'

She turned at the voice, and saw a graceful young woman with two gorgeous little children clutching her legs standing in the shade of a hut.

'Hari? It *is* you!' She ran towards her and hugged her,

tears clogging her throat. Then she crouched down and looked at the babies, twin boys with bright, curious eyes and chubby cheeks. 'They're beautiful,' she said softly, and had to swallow hard. They could so easily have died. She stroked their shoulders and they turned their heads away and clung to their mother, clearly overawed.

Gabby straightened with a smile, just as Hari patted her on the shoulder and looked towards Jed. He was coming towards them with the baby, and she took Bethany from him and handed her to Hari. The little one beamed, a great gap-toothed smile with sparkling blue eyes inherited from her father, and Hari laughed when the baby pulled her hair and explored her face with chubby little hands.

'There's somebody else to see you,' Jed said softly, and she turned just as the crowd parted and a wizened old man limped towards her.

'The *dukun*—oh, yes!' And, without any thought for cultural differences and social standing, she ran over to him and hugged him, then stood back and looked at him. 'Oh, I've wanted to see you so much,' she said, choked, and to her surprise Jed translated.

The old man's face lit up in a beaming smile that almost matched Bethany's, and he patted her shoulder and drew her into the shade under his hut. Jed, the chief and Bill followed, and the children were whisked away by the older girls and the women.

Hari brought them coffee and little cakes, and then sat and joined them, and Jed and Bill managed to act as translators. They talked about the resort, and the trees, and little Bethany, and the *dukun* took Gabby's hand in his and looked searchingly at her, then said something to Jed.

He looked puzzled, then something dawned in his

eyes. The *dukun* handed her a piece of wizened root, and she smiled in understanding and put it in her pocket.

Then it was time to go, and they bade their friends an emotional farewell. It was only later, after they were alone again and the baby was asleep, that Jed turned her in his arms.

'Was he right?'

She smiled. 'The old man? Of course.'

'We're having a boy.'

'Are we?'

'So he said. Do you need the ginger root?'

She patted her pocket. 'I'll keep it for insurance—just in case. Sue says it works better than the commercial variety. I wonder what Bethany will make of a little brother?'

Jed laughed. 'Mincemeat, if she's as bossy as you are with me. Poor lad, I feel sorry for him already.' He rested his forehead against hers. 'How about slipping out of those things and putting on something cool and refreshing?'

'Like what?'

'A *mandi*?'

She leant back in his arms and smiled. 'With you?'

He grinned wickedly. 'Of course. That's the best thing about this resort of Bill's—he's taken the best bits of everything and put them together. After we've played around in the water we can come back into the air-conditioned cabin and—well, play some more.'

She laughed softly. 'Again?'

'It is our wedding anniversary.'

'So what's your excuse every other day of the last year?'

He chuckled. 'How can it be my fault if you drive me crazy?'

She smiled and pulled off her clothes. 'Last one in the *mandi*'s a rotten egg,' she laughed over her shoulder, and ran...

ARE YOU A FAN
OF MILLS & BOON®
MEDICAL ROMANCES™?

If YOU are a regular United Kingdom buyer of Mills & Boon Medical Romances we would welcome your opinion on the books we publish.

Harlequin Mills & Boon have a Reader Panel for Medical Romances. Each person on the panel receives a questionnaire every third month asking for their opinion of the books they have read in the past three months. Everyone who sends in their replies will have a chance of winning ONE YEAR'S FREE Medicals, sent by post—48 books in all.

If you would like to be considered for inclusion on the Panel please give us details about yourself below. All postage will be free. Younger readers are particularly welcome.

Year of birth.............................Month..........................

Age at completion of full-time education.....................

Single ❑   Married ❑   Widowed ❑   Divorced ❑

Your name (print please)..

Address...

....Postcode ....

Thank you! Please put in envelope and post to:
HARLEQUIN MILLS & BOON READER PANEL,
FREEPOST SF195, PO BOX 152, SHEFFIELD S11 8TE

MILLS & BOON

Emma Darcy

The Collection

* * * *

This autumn Mills & Boon® brings you a powerful
collection of three full-length novels by an
outstanding romance author:

Always Love
To Tame a Wild Heart
The Seduction of Keira

Over 500 pages of love, seduction and intrigue.

Available from September 1998

Available at most branches of WH Smith, John Menzies,
Martins, Tesco, Asda, and Volume One

ORD INK

We are giving away a year's supply of Mills & Boon® books to the five lucky winners of our latest competition. Simply fill in the ten missing words below, complete the coupon overleaf and send this entire page to us by 28th February 1999. The first five correct entries will each win a year's subscription to the Mills & Boon series of their choice. What could be easier?

BUSINESS	**SUIT**	CASE
BOTTLE	_____	HAT
FRONT	_____	BELL
PARTY	_____	BOX
SHOE	_____	PIPE
RAIN	_____	TIE
ARM	_____	MAN
SIDE	_____	ROOM
BEACH	_____	GOWN
FOOT	_____	KIND
BIRTHDAY	_____	BOARD

C8H

Please turn over for details of how to enter ⇨

HOW TO ENTER

There are ten words missing from our list overleaf. Each of the missing words must link up with the two on either side to make a new word or words.

For example, 'Business' links with 'Suit' and 'Case' to form 'Business Suit' and 'Suit Case':

BUSINESS—SUIT—CASE

As you find each one, write it in the space provided. When you have linked up all the words, fill in the coupon below, pop this page into an envelope and post it today. Don't forget you could win a year's supply of Mills & Boon® books—you don't even need to pay for a stamp!

Mills & Boon Word Link Competition
FREEPOST CN81, Croydon, Surrey, CR9 3WZ
EIRE readers: (please affix stamp) PO Box 4546, Dublin 24.

Please tick the series you would like to receive if you are one of the lucky winners

Presents™ ❑ Enchanted™ ❑ Medical Romance™ ❑
Historical Romance™ ❑ Temptation®

Are you a Reader Service™ subscriber?   Yes ❑   No ❑

Ms/Mrs/Miss/Mr ....Initials.........................
(BLOCK CAPITALS PLEASE)

Surname...

Address ....

....

....Postcode.........................

(I am over 18 years of age)   C8H